An Orphan's Heart

LORI CRANE

Lori Crane Entertainment, Inc.
www.LoriCrane.com

This book is a work of historical fiction. Some names, characters, places, and incidents are from historical accounts. Some names, characters, places, and incidents are products of the author's imagination.

ISBN:978-0988354524
eBook ISBN:978-098835453

TABLE OF CONTENTS

1862	1
Dreams	9
1864	15
1866	19
The Trail	23
Home	37
April 4, 1872	51
Milton Carrington	63
Second Date	69
July 1874	77
A New Beginning	81
September 1875	85
Funeral	91
March 1879	95
Begging for a Ride	99
Home Again	105
Sisters	117
Aunt Mary	125
Babies and Puppies	129
Necie's Wedding Day	133
March 1884	135
Sam Meek	147
To Willie's	159
Wedding	165
June 1887	169
Twins	175
Olive Lee	179
March 1890	183
Uncle William	187
Martha Meek	189
August 1890	193
Texas Christian Advocate	197
July 15, 1986	199

1862

I don't know how long I've been standing here staring at these mounds of dirt. A few minutes? An hour? I have no idea. Time doesn't have any meaning. The funeral is over, and I'm the only one still here.

I look down the row of pine trees lining the dirt road, and see my sister Lizzie walking arm in arm with her friend David. I place my palm over my brow to shield my eyes from the glaring sun. I spot my brothers and baby sister, Necie, standing in the middle of the road, talking to Aunt Mary. I watch Aunt Mary pick up Necie and place her on her hip.

Poor little Necie doesn't even know what's happening. She keeps asking everyone where Momma is, which breaks my heart. How can she understand something like this at the age of four? I don't understand it myself. I guess it's a good thing she doesn't know we just put Momma in the ground next to Daddy.

We buried Daddy last week. Actually, *we* didn't bury him. Aunt Mary found him dead in the bed next to Momma and had my uncles sneak him out of the house while Momma was unconscious with a fever. I shiver at the thought. Aunt Mary kept us all busy in the garden while the men took Daddy away. They drove him down to the cemetery in the back of a wagon and buried him, and we didn't get to say goodbye. A mound of dirt is still piled high on his grave.

There are two mounds now.

I overheard Aunt Mary tell Aunt Martha Jane that the doctor said Momma and Daddy had typhoid fever. I don't know what that is, but it killed both my parents.

I stand alone in a forest of headstones and wonder how long I can stand here before anyone notices—probably all night. Maybe they would miss me if I didn't show up for breakfast. Maybe not.

That's the problem with being the middle child—not many people notice you. They notice the oldest: "Oh, look how big you've grown!" They notice the youngest: "Aren't you the cutest little thing?" But they don't notice you if you're in the middle. It's like being invisible.

Aunt Mary, with Necie cradled on her hip, leans her head to let Necie play with her hair for a moment. She then looks down at my brother Allen John and wraps her free arm around his shoulder, and they all start walking in the direction of Aunt Mary's house. My six-year-old little brother, Willie, walks on the same side as Necie, holding on to Aunt Mary's skirt with his dirty little fingers. I'd better follow them or I'll be left here alone in the graveyard when night falls.

I take one last look at the mounds of dirt covering the bodies of my parents, and I shed a single tear. I try to picture Daddy's face but it seems fuzzy, like a dream. I try to imagine Momma's warm smile and loving eyes, but I can't bring them into focus.

Suddenly, a black crow flies overhead and startles me with its loud "Caw!" The sound makes me jump. I wipe the tear away with the back of my hand as I turn and follow my siblings toward Aunt Mary's house.

Aunt Mary has a two-bedroom flat above her general store in town. She and Uncle Rice used to have a farm out by Daddy's, but they sold it and moved to town a couple years ago. Uncle Rice is off fighting in some war right now, but Aunt Mary has her sister—my aunt Martha Jane—staying with her to help with the store.

I was named after Aunt Martha Jane. My given name is Martha Ellen, but to avoid confusion with all the other Marthas in my family, everyone simply calls me Ellen.

Aunt Mary and Aunt Martha Jane are my daddy's sisters. He has two other sisters, but they live in different states. Aunt Susannah moved to Louisiana just before I was born, so I've never met her, but everyone talks about her all the time, so I feel like I know her.

Aunt Elizabeth lives in Alabama. I was only six when she married and moved away, but I remember her well. She's a petite, dark-haired, and beautiful woman, with the warmest smile and the prettiest sparkling blue eyes. She's one of the few people in the world who looks at me with love in her eyes, and makes me feel like I am the most important person in the world. Whenever she was around, I didn't feel so invisible.

Even though she lives far away now, she writes me often. A few times, she even invited me to come to Alabama and visit her, and I would love to. I always thought when I got older I would go visit her, but I wish I could go right now. Well, why not? Yes, maybe I'll go to Alabama. I wonder how long it takes to travel there, and I wonder who I can ask. I don't think Aunt Mary would be very pleased with the idea, so I won't ask her, but I'm sure there's somebody around who would know.

Daddy also has a bunch of brothers. The three eldest all live in different places far away, and the four youngest are off fighting in the war, so I have no uncles around here. I heard Daddy say once that the younger boys were expected home from the war before harvest, but it's now November. Most of the harvest is still sitting idle in the fields, and the boys are not home.

I stare at the road and kick pebbles as I stroll behind the rest of my siblings. I wonder what we're supposed to do now. Allen John, Lizzie, Willie, Necie, and I have all been staying with Aunt Mary for the last two weeks while some other family members tried to nurse Momma back to health. That obviously didn't work out the way they planned. Now that my parents are both gone, I wonder if we are to stay at Aunt Mary's, or if we have to move somewhere else. I hope the grown-ups don't split us up. I would hate to live without my brothers and sisters. But who would want to take in five children all at once?

It may be better for us to live with someone else, because we are more than a little cramped in the upstairs rooms at Aunt Mary's. The general store is on the first floor, and the upstairs consists of a parlor and two small bedrooms. Aunt Mary has four children of her own: Mattie, who is fourteen and best friends with my sister Lizzie; eleven-year-old

Benjamin; four-year-old Charlie; and the baby, Monroe Franklin.

My aunts and the babies share a room, and Lizzie, Mattie, Benjamin, Charlie, and I share the second room. My oldest brother Allen John sleeps on the sofa in the parlor, with Willie claiming his spot on the floor in front of the fireplace. In all, there are two women, three girls, four boys, and two babies living in a three-room flat.

It would be nice to have room to get away from the older girls. Mattie and Lizzie are annoying, inseparable teenagers who never stop talking and giggling. They sit in the corner, fixing each other's hair and whispering. They are so self-absorbed. One would think at their ages, they would help with the little ones, but they don't. They conveniently disappear when there are any chores to be done, and they always leave the cleaning and sweeping for me and Benjamin. Allen John doesn't help much, either. He has a lot of friends here in town, and when we don't have school, he likes to go hunting all day with them. I admit it's nice to have fresh meat when they bring home something, but most of the time they return empty-handed. I swear, I don't know what they do out there all day. I don't know much about hunting, but I'm sure I could bring home more than they do.

There's nothing to do here at the store. When I'm not in school, I spend most of my time just sitting on the stone steps of the front porch. Aunt Mary doesn't have cattle or a garden or a field to harvest. There's only one horse and a couple chickens out back. I think there's a hog behind the shed, too, but I haven't gone out there to look. And what would one do with a hog if there are no men around to butcher it in the fall?

I guess Aunt Mary trades goods from the store for milk and meat, but I overheard her complaining to Aunt Martha Jane that the store is getting emptier and emptier due to the war. She said people are not coming in as much as they used to, so she isn't making enough money to restock the inventory. We've been here two weeks, and I haven't seen more than a handful of customers inside. Even though Aunt Mary trades, I don't really understand how you get food if you don't go outside and gather it.

We had fruit trees and a huge garden at home. We also had a berry patch and some beehives for honey. Momma used to can everything so we never ran out, and Daddy used to kill a deer or butcher a hog in the fall and take it to Grandpa's to hang in the smokehouse. We would eat from that hog all winter as long as it wasn't Sunday. Momma always cooked chicken on Sundays. It became a joke around our house—you knew it was Sunday because Momma was cooking chicken.

I've missed our Sunday chicken the last two weeks, and I've cried myself to sleep quite a few nights because my stomach hurt so badly. I'm not sure if it's from hunger or sadness.

I've also been desperately homesick. I long to go back to our farm, back to Momma and Daddy. I want this to all be a bad dream.

After the long, long walk from the cemetery, we finally arrive at the store. I slowly climb the creaking stairs, fall facedown on my bed, and cry until I have no more tears to shed.

Nobody comes in to check on me.

I curl up in a ball, close my eyes, and fall asleep on top of the quilt. I don't know how long I doze, but I wake to the sound of everyone talking in the parlor. I smell something cooking and decide to go investigate.

When I enter the crowded parlor, no one seems to notice. I sit down at the table. Mattie and Lizzie are whispering on the sofa. Charlie and Necie are playing with some kind of toy on the floor in front of the fireplace. Allen John and Benjamin aren't here. They must be outside.

"Do you want a little stew?" Aunt Mary asks me quietly.

I nod.

She sets a full bowl in front of me and I try to eat a little bit, but once I take a few bites, I realize I don't have much of an appetite. After a while Aunt Mary asks me if I'm finished eating, though I haven't touched but a couple spoonfuls. I nod and she takes the bowl away. She then says she needs to go downstairs and help Aunt Martha Jane in the store. She asks Mattie and Lizzie to watch Necie and Charlie, but they don't stop chatting long enough to respond to her request. She looks at me with both an expression of frustration and a plea for help. I smile and nod at her. She winks at me, mouths "thank you," picks up baby Monroe, and disappears down the stairs.

I sit with my elbows on the table and my chin in my hands as I watch the children for a long time. I listen to Mattie and Lizzie talking nonstop. I wish I had someone to talk to or play with. I block the girls out as I try to figure out what we're supposed to do with our lives now. I don't think I'm supposed to be planning my future at the age of nine, but there's no one else to do it for me. If I were old enough, I'd get married and move into my own house. If I were rich enough, I'd go somewhere far away. If I were small enough, I'd crawl into a little mouse hole and never come out again.

I'm lost in thought when Aunt Martha Jane bounces up the stairs and tells me she'll mind the children and I can run along. I don't know where I'm supposed to run along to, but I nod and go into the bedroom. I put on my nightdress as the sun begins to set, and I climb into bed. I am exhausted.

The sheets are cold against my bare legs, and my feet are freezing, but I can't bring myself to care. I can't care about anything anymore. I should curl up into a ball and warm myself, but I can't will myself to move. I lie still, stare at the ceiling, and wish I would freeze from my toes to my head and die.

Dreams

The warm summer breeze feels so good on my face. I stop running for a moment, close my eyes, and tilt my head back. I breathe in the smell of wildflowers, listen to the sound of buzzing bees, and feel the warm sun on my face. I truly believe the sun can bake away any problems you have. I exhale when I hear Lizzie call my name. I open my eyes and run toward her.

Lizzie and I skip through the tall grasses, giggling and chasing brightly colored butterflies. Above our laughter, we hear Momma call our names in a singsong voice, "Lizzie. Ellen. Supper."

Lizzie and I give each other that look we both know so well—the one that says it's time for our race. Whenever Momma calls us, that's our signal to begin our race back to the house and be the first to claim her victory hug.

We don't even count to three before we start. We just take off as fast as lightning, galloping through the grasses and wildflowers. Out of the corner of my eye, I spy Lizzie trailing behind me. This victory will be mine, for there is no way she will catch me today. My legs run as quickly as a colt turned out to pasture, and

I feel invincible. When we cross the road and approach our handsome log house, I see Momma standing on the front porch. Her smile draws us closer, her eyes filled with love. She holds little Necie on her hip, her head thrown back in laughter as she awaits one of us to claim the victory hug.

When Momma laughs, Necie laughs, too. Necie's laugh sounds like fairy bells. The two of them are so beautiful. They both have the same golden blonde hair that shines like silk when the sun hits it, but Momma's hair is in a braid, and Necie's hair is tied up in curly pigtails. Everyone in my family has that same radiant blonde hair and the same blue eyes—everyone except me. For some reason, I am the ugly duckling of the family, with my dark brown hair and brown eyes. Momma told us the Ugly Duckling fable many times, but I don't think I will ever transform into a beautiful swan like in the story. It makes me sad that I don't have the same fair beauty as the rest of them, but Momma always tells me I'm beautiful.

As I reach the front porch, with Lizzie still trailing behind, Momma waves and laughs. Her face is radiant and her eyes twinkle. I hop up onto the end of the porch, jumping right over the two steps, and I run down its length toward her. When I am a few feet from her, the sunny day darkens to gray, and I feel a ghastly chill from the breeze that has abruptly turned ice cold.

I stop dead in my tracks and watch, horrified, as Momma's blonde hair turns gray right before my eyes. Behind her, everything—the magnolia bush with its white flowers, the green needles of the pine trees, and the sapphire blue sky—turns gray. I wrap my arms around myself, shielding myself from the cold air, and wonder what in the world is going on.

I wake in the room upstairs from the store. I pull the blanket tight around myself and shiver. It is freezing in here. I look over at Mattie and Lizzie, still asleep in their bed. Benjamin and Charlie are sleeping in the far bed. Very little light is coming through the window; it must be early. I remember the dream and am brought back to the reality that Momma is dead. I physically ache as I realize I won't ever again see those eyes filled with love for me.

I close my eyes, trying to bring back the dream, in hopes I can see a glimmer of her face just for a moment, but it's gone. I feel my stomach turn over and feel nauseated. I don't think I can get sick since I haven't eaten anything. I feel another wave, this one a wave of sadness. My eyes burn with tears and one spills onto my cheek. I quietly crawl out of bed, slip on my dress and shoes, and tiptoe out of the room to go find Aunt Mary.

When I enter the parlor, it's deserted. Allen John and Willie must have gone out hunting or something. I glance at Aunt Mary's door and see it ajar. She's up already, too. I notice the fire is out. That's why it's so cold in here.

I shiver, grab Willie's blanket off the floor, and wrap it around my shoulders. I walk around the sofa and pull back the curtains from the front window. The warm ray of sunshine beaming through the wavy glass feels good on my face. I think of my dream and find it strange to feel the same warmth on my face now. I stand with my eyes closed, wrapped in the blanket, and realize the sun can't bake away every problem.

I hear faint voices downstairs and look down at

the road in front of the store. There are a couple horses tied to the hitching post. I remain still and listen, but I can't make out what the voices are saying. Apparently the store has some customers, which happens rarely these days.

I turn back around and notice a large tin plate of biscuits on the dining table in the corner. I hope they're for us, but I don't think I should help myself without asking. However, I'm so hungry, I can't resist. I grab one and practically shove the whole thing in my mouth. I look around for something to wash it down with, but the water pitcher is empty. I decide to sneak downstairs and out the back door to go get a drink from the well. I wrap the blanket tighter around my shoulders and grab a cup from the cupboard. As I wait at the top of the stairs, listening to the customers saying their goodbyes, Lizzie and Mattie emerge from the bedroom.

They look ridiculous with their hair all messed up, fresh from bed. I watch them as they plop themselves down at the big table and grab for the biscuits. They whisper and giggle between themselves and don't even notice I'm standing three feet away. They look absurd as they shovel biscuits into their mouths, and somehow they never stop talking. I guess when you are a teenager you have a lot to say, even with a mouth full of biscuits. I remind myself to never become a silly teenager. They're dumb and annoying.

I ignore their stupid chatter, tiptoe down the stairs, and sneak out the back door. I lower the bucket into the well, pull it back up, dip my cup into the bucket, and take a long drink of the ice cold water.

I turn around, lean against the well, and look out

at the field. There's not a cloud in the sky, so I hope the sun will burn off this crisp chill and it'll be a warm day. I listen to the chickens cluck and the sparrows chirp. In the distance, the mist rises off the grassy field, and I watch Aunt Mary's black stallion whinny and gallop a few yards across the slope and down into the ravine. I wish Momma were here to see this. She would say how beautiful it is. I guess I will, from now on, view the scenery alone. I don't need Lizzie and Mattie to talk to me. I don't need anyone to get me a drink. I can take care of myself. I don't need anyone, not now, not ever.

I drop the blanket and the cup and run toward the field. I pick some long grasses for the horse as I approach him with my hand held open in a friendship offering. The mighty creature cautiously approaches me. I stand as still as a statue and coax him with a click of my tongue. He looks me in the eye and gently takes the grass from my hand. I slowly reach up and pet his long neck, whispering to him about how beautiful he is. He feels like velvet. I grab a large handful of his mane and pull myself up onto his back. I urge him forward by digging my heels into his side. Once he starts moving, I yell for him to go faster, and we gallop across the field as fast as his legs will carry us. I lean down over his neck, and tangle my hands tightly into his silken mane as I push him faster and faster. If I ride fast enough, maybe I can outrun the pain.

1864

The wedding is beautiful. Virginia looks like a princess, all dressed up in her ivory wedding dress, and the whole town has turned out to celebrate her wedding with a dance in our barn.

We've only lived here a month, and I love being back on a farm. The store was so cramped and boring, and I can't believe we spent over a whole year there. Here, I wake up every morning to the rooster and the smell of hay.

After Aunt Mary's husband was killed in the war, she abandoned the store and married William Jolly. His wife died of the fever last year and left him alone to raise four children. So last month, Aunt Mary and Uncle William got married and moved us all to his farm. They make a good couple, though it seems they have a million children between them. It's a full house with me and my four siblings; Uncle William's four children, including Virginia, who is the beautiful bride today; and Aunt Mary's three surviving children. Baby Monroe Franklin died of the fever last year right before his first birthday. It broke our hearts, especially Aunt Mary's. That awful fever took so many people, young and old alike, at random. It was such a frightening time, and I pray that dreadful fever is gone forever.

Getting away from the store and being on a farm again seemed to brighten everyone's spirits. Aunt Mary even began to smile as we made the last trip with a wagon full of furniture. Uncle William was happy during the move, too, but it must have been quite an adjustment for him to have twelve children in the house instead of four. Sometimes I have to laugh at his expressions; he looks a little bewildered by all the noise. I giggle at him, and I love him so much. He is a kind and gentle man who takes very good care of us all. His farm has a huge garden, lots of animals, and lots of chores to do. The days of going to bed hungry are long gone, for now we have plenty.

I think Uncle William looks very proud tonight as he struts around with his head held high. The bride is his eldest daughter, and everyone pats him on the back, saying they're happy for the newlyweds. They also tease him about becoming a grandpa soon. He chuckles and takes it all in.

I sit alone at a table and watch people laughing and smiling, which I haven't seen in such a long time. The war is taking its toll on everyone, but for tonight, everyone seems joyful. Even Aunt Mary is laughing and waltzing around the room, playing the perfect hostess. She has been so desperately sad since Monroe Franklin died. She doesn't say much about it to anyone, but I can tell her heart is forever broken.

I watch Lizzie and Mattie flirting with boys. I really don't know what they see in those boys, but maybe someday when I become a teenager, I'll figure it out. Even though I find Lizzie and Mattie utterly annoying with their incessant yakking and giggling, I do envy them a little tonight. They look so grown-up in their pretty party dresses and lacy bonnets, and I wish the boys looked at me the way they look at them. The girls are sitting at the table in the corner, batting their eyelashes at the boys. I look over and try to bat my lashes at the invisible boy next to me, but it just makes me dizzy.

As I watch the girls, Necie and Charlie run between the tables and the dancers, shrieking and laughing as they play tag with Willie. The second time they pass through, they almost run right into me. I grab their arms as they try to run past me a second time, and I tell them to stop running into people, but they don't listen. They pull away from my grasp and continue running like I don't even exist. I shake my head in frustration and decide to go outside to look at the stars.

It's such a beautiful, balmy night, but it makes me feel sad. The magnolias are in bloom, and the warm, night air is thick with their scent. The fireflies dance in the grassy field across the road. I hear a hoot owl in the distance and a bullfrog croak somewhere close by. The full moon casts a silvery light on everything, giving it a soft, blue glow.

I lean against the split-rail fence, trying to figure out why I am outside alone, feeling sorry for myself. I'm not old enough to flirt with boys. I'm not young enough to play tag. The adults are too busy talking and dancing to pay me any mind. I wish Momma were here. I would be inside, sitting at a table, chatting with people who love me.

Though I'm constantly surrounded by people, I feel so isolated. I've felt this way since Momma died a year and a half ago. Will I ever feel happy again? Will I ever feel like I belong anywhere? Or feel loved? I miss the way Momma used to look at me. I would like someone—anyone—to look at me like that. Mostly, I feel I'm just in the way. I try to be tough and brave and hold in my tears, but I can't stop them from flowing tonight. My sobs mix with the tinkling of the laughter and the joyful fiddle music coming from the barn. Tears stream down my face like a million stars falling from the sky.

1866

I crawl up into the back of the covered wagon, holding my single bag in my lap, and try to arrange my dress so it won't wrinkle too badly. My bag contains two dresses, a nightgown, and a bonnet. I left the rest of my clothes for Necie. She's growing so fast, she'll be able to wear all of them soon enough. Uncle Hays told me there's not enough room to take all my belongings, not that I have a lot, but regardless, I packed only what I thought necessary in this ugly, brown, wool bag. One of the straps is broken, so I have to carry it like a sack of potatoes.

I squeeze myself in between the mounds of furniture, pots and pans, and my cousin's belongings, and I pray this trip will go fast, because it's pretty tight and uncomfortable in here. Uncle Hays said it will take us about seven or eight days to get to Alabama if the weather cooperates. I gather the horses can't pull the wagon very fast in the mud, so if it rains, it could take up to ten days.

I've dreamt of going to Alabama for years, so when Uncle Hays told Aunt Mary he was moving there and wanted to take us children, I jumped at the opportunity. My brothers declined because they wanted to go to Texas with my other uncles, my sister Lizzie announced that she and David planned to be married, and little Necie refused to leave Aunt Mary. So, it's just me on this journey. I'm nervous to be without my siblings, but I'm excited to see Aunt Elizabeth. I take a deep breath and vow to be mature; a thirteen-year-old shouldn't act like a baby. I will not cry. I will be strong.

Uncle Hays comes into view from around the back of the wagon, pulling the leads of a horse and two mules. His gray-bearded face looks up and sees me sitting in the wagon, but his blue eyes hold no expression under the brim of his dusty hat. He quickly goes back to focusing on his job at hand.

He ties the animals to the hitch on the back. I think, "Well, that's going to be a great view. I guess I'll watch a horse and two mules for the next eight days." It takes Uncle Hays quite a while to tie them up because he has only one good arm. He took a bullet in Atlanta toward the end of the war, and came home with a right arm that doesn't work anymore.

But at least he came home, which is more than I can say for any of Daddy's other brothers. Uncle John died in battle, and the other two died of illness. At least that's what we think. We haven't heard from Uncle Timothy or Uncle Wilson since we received word they were hospitalized. It's been a year since the war ended, so more than likely they died in those hospitals. I can't understand why anyone would ever want to go to war. It took almost as many family members from us as the fever did. I close my eyes to block out the memories.

When Uncle Hays finally finishes tying the horse and mules, he looks me in the eye. He doesn't smile. I smile at him, but he remains expressionless. I suddenly feel a chill, as if I'm an intruder on his family's journey. It occurs to me maybe I should be doing something to help Aunt Loucinda get ready to leave, but I don't know what because she didn't ask me to do anything. Maybe I shouldn't go with them. Maybe I should stay here in Mississippi with Aunt Mary.

But there's nothing left for me here. Our school only goes to eighth grade, and I finished that last year. I don't have a boyfriend. Allen John and Willie are off to Texas. Lizzie and Mattie are both getting married. Necie is now eight years old, has a lot of friends at school, and is happy at Aunt Mary's. She doesn't feel the sadness and emptiness I feel. She doesn't even remember Momma. She calls Aunt Mary "Momma." I envy her.

My family is breaking apart and everyone's going their separate ways. There's only a bleak, painful, death-filled past for us here. I need to start a new life. I need to find a place where I belong, a place where I can be happy. I'm sure Aunt Elizabeth can help, but I have to get there first. I'll sit here quietly, try to stay out of the way, and in a week, I'll be in Alabama. Who knows? Maybe even Uncle Hays will get happier as we get farther away from here.

I hear little Fannie cry. She's almost three years old now and cries pretty much all the time. I hear Aunt Loucinda tell her to hush as Mary, John, and Jeff come running around the back and noisily crawl up into the wagon. Mary is nine, and the boys are eight and five.

Aunt Loucinda appears around the corner, and just hands Fannie to me without saying anything. I realize that since I'm the oldest, I'm the new caretaker for these children. For some reason, this is a startling revelation that never occurred to me until this very moment. It makes sense when I think about it, but this is hardly the promising future I envisioned when I said I wanted to move to Alabama with them. There's still time for me to change my mind, but there's no reason for me to stay. I'm sure it will all be fine once we get out on the trail. I wish we would just go already so I could stop second-guessing myself.

Aunt Loucinda lifts her wide skirt and boldly climbs into the driver's seat of the wagon. Uncle Hays sits tall on his chestnut mare. He will stay ahead of us to make sure the way is clear and passable. I hear his horse clomp around to the back of the wagon. Uncle Hays looks in and asks if we're ready and we all nod. He gives a loud whistle toward the front of the wagon, Aunt Loucinda yells to the horses, snaps the reins, and with a jolt, we are off.

The Trail

Our route to Alabama takes us on cleared, established roads, so we don't have to slow down very often. After the initial hour of excitement, the day turns to monotony as I listen to the grinding of the wheels on the dry road, feel the rocking of the wagon, and watch the landscape pass lazily by. I daydream about my new life in Alabama, and pray we make good time every day. From what I figure, we need to go at least fifteen miles a day to complete the one-hundred-ten-mile journey in the time Uncle Hays said.

As the sun begins to lower in the sky, I yell to Uncle Hays from the back of the wagon. "How far have we come today?"

"About thirteen miles so far," he yells back.

Between the monotony of the travel and Fannie's constant crying, my nerves are shot for today. The thought of six more days of this almost makes me cry myself. Aunt Loucinda says little Fannie may have a bellyache, or perhaps she's teething. Even though Aunt Loucinda has raised three children, mostly alone because Uncle Hays was off fighting in the war, I don't think she has any idea why Fannie is upset.

Fannie cries pretty much all the time, so I don't know how anyone could tell the difference between a bellyache and a new tooth. No matter how I try to soothe the child, it does no good. I bounce her and rock her and sing to her, but as soon as she dozes off, she twitches or jumps, and the crying begins all over again.

By the time we finally stop for the night, I am utterly drained from being with a crying toddler all day, and I don't think I have any hearing left. I stiffly climb down from the wagon and am happy to hand her back to her mother. I stretch my back in an attempt to stand up straight. I didn't realize sitting all day would make one inflexible.

Uncle Hays builds a fire and Aunt Loucinda warms up leftover stew. We sit around the fire and enjoy a modest meal, dipping pieces of stale bread in our bowls. We then help Uncle Hays put up a tent and crawl in for the night. Uncle Hays tells us to get right to sleep because we'll head out early tomorrow morning. He says by tomorrow night, we should be close to the Tombigbee River. We'll follow that all the way up to Pickens County, so we'll have a good supply of water for the rest of the journey. Until then, we have enough water stored for us and the animals to be comfortable.

Uncle Hays, Aunt Loucinda, and Fannie sleep in the wagon, and the rest of us curl up in the tent. I listen to the crickets as I doze off. The ground is hard and the air is chilly, but I am too tired to care. I'm emotionally weary from the nervousness of leaving my family, mentally exhausted from dealing with Fannie all day, and physically sore from sitting in the cramped wagon. I have no trouble falling asleep.

I hear a loud caw of a crow and open my eyes. I can't believe it's light already. It feels like I just fell asleep ten minutes ago. I stretch and feel a pain between my shoulder blades. I come to the conclusion that riding in a wagon or sleeping on the ground, or both, is not good for one's back. Aunt Loucinda pops her head into the tent and tells us to get up so we can get on the road.

It's cold and damp, and my clothes are sticking to me like I bathed in them. I get a shiver, feel goose bumps on my arms, and my hands and feet are freezing. I hope it warms up quickly. I pack up the blankets and help the children pack the tent as Aunt Loucinda warms up some sowbelly and cornbread for us. The breakfast is deliciously hot and delightful. I smell coffee and look around but don't see any. I assume Uncle Hays and Aunt Loucinda already drank all that was made, so I try to forget about it. Following breakfast, we wash the dishes and pack them away. Then we take our respective places and return to the trail.

No sooner does the wagon start moving then Fannie starts crying. I decide to not let it bother me today, as there is nothing I can do about it. I hum, though it's more to drown out her cries than soothe her, and I rock her as I watch the landscape pass at a snail's pace.

As the sun starts to rise and the air becomes warmer, I sit in the spot where I can feel the beams on my face. The inside of the wagon begins to heat up, and the steady rocking finally puts Fannie to sleep. I am thankful for the quiet.

Even though I'm achy, still a little damp, and pretty miserable, I can't help but notice how beautiful the landscape is becoming. It's so open, you can see all the way to the horizon. At home, you can see only as far as the row of pine trees on the other side of the road. The sweeping backdrop is stunning as we slowly pass large fields of corn and cotton and a few quaint little farmhouses. I'm amazed at the difference twenty miles can make, and I feel my spirits lift at the thought of my new and promising life.

At midday, we stop for an early supper at a little town called York. I have never seen so many people scurrying back and forth on their way to somewhere. They all seem to be in such a hurry and at first I don't know why. Then I hear it—the deafening whistle of a mighty train announcing its arrival. I didn't notice the train depot next door to the boarding house or the tracks outside the windows. The arriving train hisses and spits steam as it slows its way to a stop right in front of me. Through the glass, I watch travelers exit the train, and I overhear bits and pieces of their conversations. They just arrived from Atlanta. I don't know how far that is, but it must be a long way if you have to take a train.

There were train tracks next to Aunt Mary's store, so I have seen and heard trains many times, but I guess I thought they were only for transporting produce, cotton, cattle, and goods. I never considered the possibility that people could ride them, too. I'm in awe of the travelers from Atlanta—men dressed in suits and vests, women in lacy, high necklines and fancy bonnets. Some even carry ruffled umbrellas. They look so glamorous. I vow that I will one day take a train to a distant place. Not to Atlanta. No, somewhere no one has ever heard of—an exotic place that holds a promise of fascinating people and a thrilling adventure.

Uncle Hays buys a newspaper from the front desk and looks through it while we eat, but he doesn't share any of the news with us, though it doesn't matter much to me because I'm obsessed with watching the people outside. I see a woman smile as a handsome young man picks up her ornate bag, and they climb into a buggy led by two beautiful white horses. They look at each other so happily, and are obviously in love. I wonder who they are and where they're going, and I feel envious of their happiness. I will be that happy someday. Yes, someday.

When we finish supper, we stuff our pockets with as many leftovers as can fit so we can eat them later when we stop for the night. As we walk back to our wagon, I turn around again and again to admire the train. I don't know anyone who has ever ridden on one, and I promise myself I will be the first to try it.

As the sun begins to set, we reach the Tombigbee River, just as Uncle Hays predicted. Even in the dim light of dusk, it is breathtaking here. The distant horizon has given way to deep green ferns and tall trees lining the banks of the river, and the air is thick with a musty, fishy scent. We have a creek at home, but its banks can't compare with the ones surrounding this lush and beautiful river.

After we stop, Uncle Hays tells us the story of the Tombigbee. It's a Choctaw Indian name that means coffin maker. I'm a bit confused; I don't understand what a coffin maker has to do with a river.

"Are we going to cross it? It looks deep and I never learned to swim," I ask nervously. The more I think about it, the more coffin maker starts to make sense.

"We're going to follow the river up about eighty miles and cross at the shallow, narrow part further north," Uncle Hays says.

I'm not very excited about that plan. I wish there was a bridge we could cross.

We put up our tent for the night, and Uncle Hays tells us we'll do some fishing in the morning before we set out for the day. I assume that means we're having fish for supper tomorrow. I ponder the river, the train, and the little town of York as I watch the setting sun turn the reflection on the water to match the soft pink and golden clouds in the sky. All in all, it was a good day.

As we set out on day three, we pass wonders like I have never seen. There are riverboats floating on the water and quaint log houses on the banks. I wonder what it would be like to wake up to the river every morning instead of to the rooster on the farm. I observe people fishing and washing clothes on the banks and waving hello to the passing boats.

I've never seen a boat, much less been on one. These are all made of wood, some with tall masts for sails, some powered only by a lone oarsman. Most are flatboats, carrying produce and goods up and down the river, but a few are so small, they can carry only two people. I wonder how they can look so solid and yet not sink.

When we stop on the banks to eat and let the animals rest for a while, I watch some men float some logs down the river, another thing I've never seen. They actually stand on top of the logs and push other logs with poles. I don't know how they do that without falling off and drowning. I watch them until they float out of sight.

I turn my attention to Aunt Loucinda and ask her to tell me about Alabama. From what I understand, she was born and raised there and her family still lives there, so she must have some great stories.

"Well, don't expect to sit around and do nothing all day like you have been doing at your aunt Mary's. We raise hogs in Alabama and hog-raisin' is hard work," she snaps.

I don't really understand why she's using that stern tone of voice, so I try to lighten the mood. "Oh, I'm anxious to help and learn about hog farming."

I smile at her, but she doesn't smile back. I swallow hard, wondering once again if I should have stayed in Mississippi.

When we finish eating, we clean up the dishes and move out. I have been so mesmerized by the river and its goings-on, I didn't even notice the sky beginning to fill with threatening rain clouds.

"We have to go as far as we can this evening," Uncle Hays yells to Aunt Loucinda.

I don't know what her response was, if any, but he continues, "If it rains as much as it looks like it may, the wagon will be too bogged down in the mud tomorrow. We'll be lucky to travel at all."

I look out the front and see his face. His brow is wrinkled and his jaw is tight. I realize I'm not the only one who is anxious to get to Alabama.

Just as it gets dark, we stop and struggle in the blackness to make camp for the night. It couldn't have happened a moment sooner. The minute we crawl into the tent, thunder fills the nighttime silence and the sky opens up. Over the pounding of the downpour, I hear Fannie cry from the nearby wagon each time the thunder sounds. Little Jeff snuggles up close to me in the tent. By the way he burrows under the blanket and grips my arm, I can tell the thunder is making him nervous. I pull him close and wrap my arm around him. Raindrops start soaking through the tent and onto the blanket, and I feel so discouraged by the storm, my tears start to flow. I hold Jeff tightly to me as I move my head to the side to avoid the drips. I don't even bother to wipe the tears away.

As Uncle Hays warned yesterday, day four is a complete washout. He and Aunt Loucinda are both cranky due to Fannie keeping them up all night, and the horses can barely pull the wagon through the thick mud. It doesn't seem like we're moving at all; I'm sure I could walk faster than this. I think again that I should have stayed in Mississippi, but it's too late to change my mind now. I just need to focus on remaining positive.

"Uncle Hays?" I yell out the back of the wagon.

He slows down and rides up behind us.

"How far do we have to go?" I ask.

"You need to stop being so impatient, girl. We will get there when we get there," he barks as rain drips from the brim of his hat onto his legs.

I think that *I'm* not the one who needs to stop being impatient, but I don't dare say it out loud. I plant myself back in my seat and hold sleeping Fannie close to my chest.

During the night the rain finally tapers off, and we wake to the birds chirping and the sun shining. I hope the road is dry enough to make some progress today, but find that is not the case. We move faster than yesterday, but not by very much.

After a few hours of boredom and stillness, I begin to doze off, when suddenly the wagon lurches to the left and we're all thrown from our seats. My heart pounds in my chest. Aunt Loucinda yells for Uncle Hays, and the horses whinny as they rear up and pull from the wagon. I don't know what has happened, but I know it isn't good.

I hear Uncle Hays ride up to the front of the wagon, but I can't see anything except the horse and mules tied to the back. The wagon is leaning to the left.

"I expected something like this after all that rain. Damn!" says Uncle Hays.

"Hays! The children!" Aunt Loucinda chides in a hushed tone.

"Let's set up camp and I'll ride back to York for a wheel," he says.

He rides around to the back of the wagon and orders us all out.

"Did we break a wheel?" I ask.

He doesn't answer me. He's off his horse and crawling under the wagon.

Fannie begins to cry, but Aunt Loucinda doesn't take her from me. She's unhitching the horses and moving them off the road. I don't know what to do, but figure it's best to keep the children out of the way. I take them all to a nearby clearing and order them to gather wood for a fire. They're good children and do exactly as they're told. Uncle Hays takes one of the mules with him back to York to purchase a new wheel. He promises to return before nightfall.

I'm sad to be stuck once again, but relieved we didn't make much progress yesterday so Uncle Hays doesn't have too far to go. I hope he can fix a wagon wheel with his one good arm. I look around, thinking this would not be a good place to stay for an extended time.

We set up the tent and cook some supper. I take Fannie in the tent with us for the night, and leave Aunt Loucinda sitting on the front of the wagon with a shotgun in her hands.

When I wake on day six, I hear Uncle Hays working on the wagon. The children are all sleeping, so I quietly crawl out of the tent to see if we'll be able to travel today. Fortunately, Uncle Hays is able to replace the wheel, and the road has finally dried out. I hope we'll make up for lost time.

While we travel, the dull scenery begins to drag. I am bored and achy, and I could just scream out of sheer frustration. I'm sick of being sweaty and muddy during the day, and cold and damp at night, and I am so tired of this crying baby. I pray nonstop we are getting close. Uncle Hays said in the beginning that it would take seven or eight days without rain, so I try to do the math in my head to pass the time. Since the rain and broken wheel slowed us down and today is day six, I'm hoping we'll arrive by the day after tomorrow.

I feel a renewed energy when I wake up to the birds chirping on day seven. We are close. But for some reason, Uncle Hays and Aunt Loucinda don't seem to be in any hurry to get started. I sit patiently in the back of the wagon with my bag on my lap, waiting to leave. Finally I hear a swishing sound that I know is Aunt Loucinda's skirt approaching the back of the wagon. I assume she's coming around to hand Fannie to me, but when I see her, she isn't holding my little cousin. She places her hands on her hips and stares at me. I raise my eyebrows questioningly and wait for her to say something.

"What are you doing?" she asks.

"I, um, am just ready to go. Are we leaving soon?"

"Oh my goodness," she exclaims and rolls her eyes at me.

"I'm sorry. Am I doing something wrong?"

"Child, it is Sunday. We do not work on the Sabbath. We will not travel on the Sabbath. Didn't your parents or your aunt Mary raise you right?" she snips.

How dare she say anything bad about my parents! It's all I can do to maintain a civil tone with her. "I didn't know we wouldn't travel on Sunday. I'm sorry, Aunt Loucinda," I reply, but I don't move from my space in the back of the wagon because she's blocking the exit.

"Well?" she snaps.

"Ma'am?" I ask, not knowing what she expects me to do now.

"Get out of the wagon, young lady. We are going to have Sunday service. Just because we're not at our church today doesn't mean we can behave like we're not Christian."

"Yes, ma'am." I place my bag down and crawl toward the back of the wagon.

I try to climb down without touching her, but she's standing so close, it's almost impossible. Somehow I manage to squeeze out of the back without knocking her down. When I land on the ground, I turn to her for further instructions. She shakes her head and walks away.

I'm distraught at the thought of spending an extra day on the trail, but I'm so angry at her remarks, I don't know whether to cry or scream. I think either will only make her think worse of me. I will get to Alabama. I will see Aunt Elizabeth. That is all that matters.

We all gather in the clearing and sit in a semicircle, with Fannie on Aunt Loucinda's lap, and Jeff on my lap, as Uncle Hays reads from the Bible and gives a sermon that is more a lecture to the children about how they should respect their parents. He addresses doing their chores, minding their manners, and not talking back. The children sit like stones, not fidgeting, not wiggling. They don't seem like real children at all. Something feels very strange to me, but I can't put my finger on it.

My father and mother did not raise our family this way. They were very warm and affectionate. They always hugged and smiled and laughed and played. I miss my father's hugs and the love that radiated from my mother's eyes. Aunt Mary did not run her family this way, either. She was not as warm as my mother, but then again, she lost so many family members over a short amount of time, I think she was just sad. She was, however, a very devoted mother and was kind and gentle. I never once heard her raise her voice or snap at anyone. I don't understand why this family is run like the children are little soldiers. I don't like it, but I know I need to remain quiet and obedient until I get to my new home.

Aunt Elizabeth's will be different. She is loving and always has a smile on her face. I can't wait to feel her arms around me, giving me a real hug. It will be so nice to be with someone who's genuinely happy to be with me. I plan on spending a lot of time with her, and hope her house is close to Uncle Hays's so I can go over there all the time. Well, at least when I'm not minding children and hogs.

Finally, on the afternoon of day eight, we cross the Tombigbee. Uncle Hays was right; it is shallow. It only covers the bottom half of the wheels, and the horse and mules walk right through it. I watch the mules splashing and listen to Aunt Loucinda urging the horses on. I hear Uncle Hays snap a whip. I'm still terrified of being in the middle of the mighty river. I have horrifying images of overturning and plunging to my death among Aunt Loucinda's pots and pans. I hold my breath until we are safely on the other side.

We must be getting close now, but I don't dare ask. It was two days to the river, which was about thirty miles, and Uncle Hays said we'd follow the river for eighty miles, so that's one hundred ten miles total. I eye every farmhouse we pass and cross my fingers that one of them belongs to Aunt Elizabeth.

After a few hours of passing field after field and farmhouse after farmhouse, we stop.

"Here we are," Uncle Hays announces into the back of the wagon.

The children all jump out and run around in circles, yelling and waving their arms. I laugh at their silly behavior, and cringe at the same time, knowing one of the adults will have something negative to say about it. But the remarks don't come, and I'm thankful. It has been eight days of cold, damp, crying-baby misery, but finally, we are here. I want to jump up and down with the children. I climb out the back with Fannie in my arms, and look at my new home for the first time.

I'm not very impressed with the outside of the house, but at least it's a real house with a roof. It's downtrodden and could use some nails and a hammer. A couple of the shutters are hanging loose, and the front porch looks as if it might fall down any moment. But I'm sure Uncle Hays will fix it up nicely as time allows.

I notice a chimney above the roofline on the right side of the house, and am overjoyed at the thought of a warm fireplace. I also see a pump handle sticking out of the ground on the left side of the yard, and am thrilled to have fresh water available. I can't wait to rinse a week's worth of grime off of me, wash my dresses, and sleep in a real bed.

Home

The interior of the downtrodden house isn't quite as bad as the exterior. The worn and weathered log home contains a parlor, a dining room, and three bedrooms. Aunt Loucinda and I immediately begin sweeping the floors and removing the cobwebs, so we can bring in the bedding before nightfall.

We spend the next three days unpacking the wagon and placing everything in its proper place, while Uncle Hays works on repairing the broken shutters and the fences out back that will eventually contain the hogs. Aunt Loucinda orders me around relentlessly, and every time I place something in a cabinet or a drawer, she chastises me for putting it in the wrong spot. I don't know how there could possibly be a right spot when she hasn't lived here before to know the difference, but she obviously knows where she wants things. Or maybe she's just trying to make me miserable. She complains so much, I feel more like an inept farmhand than a niece. All I know is that I need to quietly do what I am told until I can see Aunt Elizabeth.

The days slowly pass and we finally have the house in working order. Even though it wasn't easy,

I'm very proud of our accomplishment, and feel a weight lifted off my shoulders.

We sit down to supper at the big table, and Uncle Hays says, "George is going to run a wagon full of hogs down here tomorrow."

Uncle George is married to Aunt Elizabeth and is brother to Aunt Loucinda. I can hardly contain myself at the thought of finally seeing my aunt.

"It's about time," replies Aunt Loucinda, placing the last supper dish on the table and taking her seat.

"Is Aunt Elizabeth coming with him?" I ask eagerly.

"Ellen, please do not interrupt," Aunt Loucinda chastises.

I lower my eyes to the table, and sit quietly and listen as they continue their conversation about hogs, fences, and Uncle George's lack of timeliness, but I never receive an answer to my question.

After we finish washing the dishes and putting the little ones to bed, I find Uncle George on the porch, smoking his pipe, and I again ask if Aunt Elizabeth will be coming tomorrow. He takes his pipe out of his mouth and is starting to answer when we're startled by a howl in the distance. Uncle Hays jumps out of his chair, leaving it rocking back and forth as he grabs his rifle and disappears into the darkness.

When he doesn't return after an hour, I give up and go to bed.

The moment I hear the birds chirping outside and see the sky lightening out the window, I spring out of bed and put on the least dirty of my three dresses, in hopes of seeing my aunt today. I have never been so excited about anything in my entire life. I help make breakfast for the children and tidy up around the house, and I follow that with searching for anything to do to pass the time. I don't think a morning has ever dragged by so slowly. I sweep and dust and clean windows. I even shovel the ashes out of the fireplace. I notice out of the corner of my eye Aunt Loucinda watching me, but I don't care what she thinks, and she doesn't say anything.

When I hear horses pull up the road, I squeal and run toward the front door, throw it open, and run onto the porch. Clomping into the drive are a couple big draft horses pulling a large wagon full of baby hogs. When the wagon comes to a halt, I watch Uncle George climb down, but Aunt Elizabeth is not with him.

My bottom lip quivers, and I feel hot tears well up in my eyes. I step off the porch to greet Uncle George and to ask after Aunt Elizabeth, but at that very moment, Uncle Hays appears from around the corner of the house and greets Uncle George. They shake hands and begin inspecting the hogs, and taking them one by one around back to put in the pen. Neither of my uncles notices me standing there. I feel tears trickle down my cheeks and think this is the most awful day ever. Why didn't she come see me? Am I to stay here and be treated like a maid to my aunt Loucinda and a caretaker for her children for the rest of my life? I did not come all the way to Alabama for this. I could have stayed in Mississippi and remained sad. It's painfully obvious I don't belong here anymore than I belonged there. Aunt Elizabeth is never going to come for me. Maybe I should go back to Aunt Mary's house, but I have no idea how to do that. I run across the road into the woods, sit down at the base of a tall pine tree, and sob.

A few more days go by without a visit from Aunt Elizabeth. I don't understand why she hasn't come see me yet. I feel so alone around here. Maybe I'll feel better if I get out of this house and meet some people. We haven't attended church since we've been here because we've been so busy setting up the house, and they only have service once a month here, but this morning, we are going. The journey to the church lifts my spirits considerably. Even though I'm nervous about meeting new people, the bright morning sun and the promise of a new day brings a small smile to my face.

When Uncle Hays pulls the wagon up to the front of the fieldstone church, we all climb down and are immediately greeted by a family who obviously knows Uncle Hays and Aunt Loucinda. They shake his hand warmly and hug her, which gives me a shiver. Why would anyone do that? My aunt and uncle do not acknowledge me or introduce me to the new family. I sigh, wondering if I am going to meet anyone at all if I stay by my aunt's side.

We sit toward the back of the small chapel, which gives me the opportunity to view most of the people. There are many couples with small children sitting on their laps and fidgeting in the pews. Mary, John, and Jeff do not fidget. I still don't understand why these children do not act like children. Fannie is asleep in my aunt's arms.

I glance around, looking for someone my age, and spot two girls sitting a couple rows in front of me. They keep turning around, looking over their shoulders at me, and I know they're whispering about me. It's a little unnerving to see them stealing glances, but I decide that when the service ends, I will introduce myself. They're probably just wondering who I am. For now, I ignore them and continue my visual search of the room. I wonder if Aunt Elizabeth will be in attendance, but maybe she and her family live too far away to attend this church. I don't see her.

Following the service, everyone enjoys fellowship outside on the front lawn. I slip away from my aunt and search for the two girls. I don't have to look far; they're standing by the driveway, eyeing me and whispering. The blonde is wearing a beautiful dark golden dress and bonnet that not only match the color of her hair perfectly, but look very, very expensive. The brunette is equally as beautiful in an emerald green dress with lace trim, her hair tied up in ribbons of the same color. The green matches her eyes, as well as the color of my envy of her gorgeous dress. I rub my palms down the front of my drab-brown wool dress, smoothing down the wrinkles and wiping the moisture from my hands at the same time. I take a deep breath to steady my nerves and walk toward them.

"Hello," I say.

"Hey," the blonde says, almost smiling, but not quite.

"Who are you?" asks the brunette in a friendly tone.

"I'm Ellen. I just moved here from Mississippi."

"Those your parents?" asks the blonde, nodding

toward my aunt and uncle.

"No," I say quickly. "That's my aunt and uncle."

"You live with them? Where are your momma and daddy?" the blonde asks, in a tone that gives me the feeling she'll enjoy the presumption of being better than me if she has proof I don't have rich parents like she obviously does.

I don't really know what to say. Can you just blurt out to total strangers that your parents are dead? There's not much else to say, but I'm not comfortable giving them that information. "They're not here. I live with my aunt and uncle."

"Oh," says the brunette. "We've neglected our manners. I'm Bethany and this is Sue." She gestures toward the blonde.

"It's very nice to meet you both. Do you live close by?" I try to make polite conversation, as well as find out if these girls could become my friends.

"Yes," answers Bethany. "A couple miles down that way." She points to her left. "How about you?"

"I'm a couple miles that way." I point in the opposite direction. I don't have a horse or wagon to travel to their homes, so I guess a friendship with them will not be possible. I'm not sure it's a great loss, though.

"Are you going to attend our school?" asks Sue.

"School? Um, no, I've finished school."

"Finished? You are so lucky. We have to go every day," Bethany complains, rolling her eyes.

Sue perks up. "Have you met any of the boys?"

"No." I haven't even thought about meeting boys. I've solely been focused on staying out of Aunt Loucinda's way and hoping to see Aunt Elizabeth.

"Too bad," Sue continues. "There are some

handsome boys around here." She giggles and looks around. I figure she wants to show me some of the handsome boys, but pouts when she doesn't see any.

It's obvious she's a little boy crazy. I assume since they haven't finished school yet, they're younger than I and probably a little too young to be looking at boys, but I attempt to fit in. "I'd like to meet some handsome boys. My uncle is raising hogs, and that's all I've seen for weeks and weeks." I giggle, but it comes out a little forced and phony.

They exchange a glance with each other. I'm not sure what it means.

"Well, we have to go now," says Bethany. "It was a pleasure meeting you. Maybe we'll see you again next month." She smiles and pulls Sue toward their waiting wagon, which is almost as fancy as their dresses.

"Sure. Next month." I smile and nod.

They giggle as they walk away, and I hear one of them say, "Raising hogs?" They laugh.

"There you are!" Aunt Loucinda barks, drawing me out of my reverie. "Who were those girls?"

"Sue and Bethany. They live down the road that way."

"It's time to go," she snaps. She marches away, carrying Fannie toward Uncle Hays in the waiting wagon. We all climb aboard and head toward home.

Except for church once a month, I don't speak with anyone at all. I don't go anywhere, I don't see anyone. I mope around for weeks, wondering if I made the right choice coming here. I do chores, help with the children, and I try to stay as quiet and out of the way as possible. I spend most of my free time walking through the dark pines across the road from the house. No one ever comes out there, so I can pout and cry all I want in solitude.

I tend to spend more time doing laundry than anything else. These children have a lot of clothes to wash. Since Aunt Loucinda has announced she's pregnant, I have come to the conclusion doing laundry is dangerous for a pregnant woman.

On this day, like I do every day, I'm carrying the heavy load of laundry toward the house after pulling it off the line. I reach the end of the front porch and hear a horse and wagon coming up the road, so I place the basket on the porch and wait to see who is in the wagon, even though I don't know a soul around here. I almost scream at the sight. It's Aunt Elizabeth!

When she sees me, her face lights up with the biggest smile I have ever seen. She hasn't changed a bit in almost nine years. She jumps down from the wagon while it's still moving, and holds up her skirt as she runs to me and takes me in her arms. She gives me the longest hug anyone has given me in years. I melt in her embrace and start to cry like a baby. I vaguely notice Uncle George park the wagon and walk around the back of the house, probably looking for Uncle Hays. I don't care about him; I'm just overjoyed to see my beautiful aunt.

"What is wrong, sweet Ellen?" she asks as she pushes my hair out of my face and gazes into my eyes.

"I thought you would never come." Her eyes are filled with such love, the same love I used to see in my mother's eyes. "I am so happy to see you," I blubber as I wrap my arms around her waist.

"Well, I'm happy to see you, too, sweetheart." She hugs me even harder. "I haven't seen you since you were six years old." She pushes me away and looks me up and down. "But you look exactly the same, just more grown up, and you're the same height as me now. You used to be this tall." She holds up her hand next to her waist. "But I would still know you anywhere. How old are you now?"

"I just turned fourteen." I wipe the tears from my cheeks and smile at her. My heart is racing and feels like it's going to pound out of my chest.

"Fourteen? Oh, my! You are so beautiful. Look at you. I see your momma and your daddy in you." She wipes the remaining tears from my face. Her eyes twinkle as she holds my chin up so she can look at me.

She takes my hand, pulls me over to the porch steps, and sits down. "Come sit next to me and let's catch up. Now, where are your brothers and sisters?" she asks excitedly.

"Lizzie is getting married to David Morrow. Do you know him?"

"Yes, I remember the Morrow family, but I can't imagine our little Lizzie as a married woman. Oh my goodness, how time flies." She shakes her head and slaps both hands on her thighs as she talks.

"And Allen John and Willie moved to Texas with Momma's uncles. We got a letter from them when they arrived, and they said they're doing well, but it took them over three weeks to get there by wagon train," I continue.

"I can imagine. Texas? That's unbelievable. What about Necie?"

"Necie is still staying with Aunt Mary. She's nine years old now."

"Nine? My, my, so much time has passed. She was just a newborn the last time I saw her. Well, I'm glad to hear everyone is doing well. You have to come over and see my children. I have John, Cornelia, Will, Laura, and Beulah." She counts them out on her fingers as she says their names. "They range in age from nine to one. It's a house full." She smiles a glorious smile, and I can tell she loves those children more than anything in the world. I realize the reason she hasn't come to see me sooner: she's a busy mother, probably the best mother any child could have. That endears her to me even more. I want to stay in her presence forever and ever.

"I would love to come see them."

"Well, do you want to come and stay with me for a while? We have room for you, and I'll ask your aunt if that will be all right," she says.

"Really? I would love nothing better than that. I don't know if she will let me go, but I would love it if you'd ask." I smile, feeling a little hopeful for the first time in months.

"All right, you stay right here, and I'll be right back," she says as she rises and disappears through the screen door.

I hear her and Aunt Loucinda greet each other. Aunt Elizabeth warmly calls her Sister. Aunt Loucinda sounds cold as always. I hope Aunt Loucinda is in a good mood and will allow me to go. I sit still, struggling to overhear their conversation.

Aunt Elizabeth asks, "Lucy, would you mind if Ellen came to stay with me for a little while? I'd love to spend some time with her and catch up on everything."

Lucy? I've never heard anyone call my aunt Lucy before. It certainly doesn't fit her. I hold my breath and await the reply.

"You want to take Ellen home with you?" A cold chuckle echoes through the open door. "I would appreciate it if you would. I'm having another child soon and we really don't have the room to keep her here much longer. I'll tell you something, though. She's not worth much, pretty slow and lazy, if you ask me."

Did she really just say that? Doesn't she know I'm sitting right here on the porch and can hear every word she's saying? My eyes fill with tears and my chest fills with both pain and anger. Why would she be so mean? I don't want to hear any more of their conversation. The tears roll down my cheeks as I stand up and run across the road to the woods. I wish my mother were here to make all of this go away. My mother wouldn't allow Aunt Loucinda to be so unkind. I am not slow, and I am certainly not lazy. There's just no way to do anything right around her.

I wander around the woods for a long time, taking my frustrations out on the trees by hitting them with sticks as hard as I can. When one stick breaks, I search the underbrush until I find another, then swing it at the nearest tree. Finally exhausted, void of tears, and knowing I must face my fate, I head back to the house to see what their decision is. I'm sure Aunt Elizabeth doesn't want me now that she thinks I'm slow and lazy.

When I cross the road, Uncle George and Aunt Elizabeth are sitting on the porch steps. Uncle Hays and Aunt Loucinda are nowhere to be seen.

"There you are!" Aunt Elizabeth stands up. "I thought we were going to have to leave without you."

"You mean I can go with you?"

"Of course, and we're happy to have you." She smiles warmly.

Uncle George looks at me and smiles, but it's more obligatory because I'm his wife's niece. I shyly smile back at him, wondering if he likes me or not. He rises from the steps and heads toward the wagon.

"Are we going right now? I'll go pack my things," I say excitedly as I hurry up the steps and reach for the door.

"Loucinda already packed your things," Uncle George says as he checks the reins on the horses.

I stop and whirl around to face him. "She packed for me?" I ask, slightly annoyed that she would touch my things, even though there are only two dresses, a nightgown, and a bonnet, but more upset that she seems to be happy to get rid of me as quickly as possible.

"Yep," he says as he climbs up on the wagon, ready to leave.

"Why don't you run in and say goodbye," Aunt Elizabeth says. She heads to the wagon also.

"Hurry up. It's going to be dark soon," Uncle George adds.

I hurry into the house and hug all the children. I then go out the back door to find Uncle Hays. He's in his usual place in the muddy hog pen.

I run up to the fence. "Goodbye, Uncle Hays. I'm going to Aunt Elizabeth's for a while."

"All right, then. Goodbye," is all he says.

He doesn't turn toward me. He doesn't come give me a hug. I don't think he even cares that I'm leaving. I watch him for a moment and realize there is nothing else to wait for, so I head back into the house to find Aunt Loucinda.

I find her in one of the bedrooms, putting clean sheets on a bed. I knock on the half-open door and wait for her to beckon me.

"I brought the basket of laundry in from the front porch. I thought you had already gone," she says curtly.

"Oh, I'm sorry about that, but I wouldn't leave without saying goodbye," I say as I enter the room.

"Well, goodbye. I'll see you again sometime," she says. She doesn't stop making the bed and doesn't look up at me. I assume she won't give me a hug, so I leave the room, sighing that it's over, at least for a while.

Riding in the wagon with Aunt Elizabeth and Uncle George is a whole different experience than traveling to Alabama with Uncle Hays. Uncle George relates stories of the people who live on each farm as we pass. Aunt Elizabeth chatters on and on about their farm and their children. I feel my optimism growing as I distance myself from Aunt Loucinda. I vow to be the best houseguest I can be, so I can stay with Aunt Elizabeth forever.

As the sun sets, we pull up in front of their house. It's a modest yet cute house sitting very close to the road. There is room only for the wagon between the front porch and the road. I look around the property but can't see much of the land due to dusk overshadowing everything, but from what I can see, it looks nice enough.

Aunt Elizabeth's children all come running out onto the porch to greet us. They are the cutest little things, and I feel welcome already. Eight-year-old Cornelia carries baby Beulah in her arms, and gives me a huge smile. Laura, who is two, hides behind Cornelia, nervous about a stranger approaching the house. Nine-year-old John and six-year-old William say hello, then fight over who gets the privilege of carrying my bag into the house. Uncle George yells at them to act like they have some manners, and they both apologize to me. John grabs my bag and by the time they hit the porch, they're fighting again, with William trying to grab it from him. Aunt Elizabeth just shakes her head and rolls her eyes at me, and I giggle.

April 4, 1872

It's April 4th! Happy birthday to me. I wake to the sound of the girls giggling in the other room. I imagine they're up to something. I lie in bed a few moments and enjoy the promise of a wonderful day ahead. I'm grateful and happy for everything in my life, especially Aunt Elizabeth. I can't believe I have been here for five years now, and am so thankful for the home she has provided me, along with the five beautiful children who were here when I arrived, and Albert and Robert, three and two years old, who arrived later. They are handfuls, and I don't think Aunt Elizabeth could manage all this work on her own, so I am more than happy to lend a hand. Lately she looks so tired and her color is a little off. I don't think she's very healthy, and I'm worried about her. I often see her stop what she's doing and grimace. When I ask her if she's feeling all right, she always smiles and says, "Of course, I'm fine!" but I don't believe her. There's not much I can do except help her with the house and the children so she doesn't overexert herself.

I stretch my toes under the covers and take a deep breath. Time to get this day started. I lift my head, glance around the cozy room, and notice all the children have already gotten up. I can't believe I didn't hear them this morning. I crawl out of bed and dress in the new light blue dress Aunt Elizabeth made for me. I unbraid my hair, hurriedly run my fingers through it, and put it back into a braid. I move as quickly as I can, for I need to help the children get ready for school.

When I enter the parlor, Aunt Elizabeth and all of the children are waiting for me with big grins.

"We let you sleep in," hollers Laura, who is missing a couple teeth in the front and looks silly when she grins.

"Yeah, sleep in," says Beulah.

The smell of hotcakes, maple syrup, and pork sausage is so inviting, my stomach growls. Cornelia places a plate on the table and gestures for me to sit down. They all wish me a happy birthday, and Aunt Elizabeth comes up behind me, wraps her arms around my neck, and gives me a long hug.

"We will have a grand celebration for you this evening," she says, "but for now, enjoy your breakfast. The children all pitched in and made it for you special."

I haven't had a birthday party since my ninth birthday, right before my parents died. Momma made my favorite supper that night—chicken and dumplings. I can't believe Aunt Elizabeth is going to throw a party for me. My eyes start to fill with tears. I try to blink them away as I smile.

"No, no, no tears on your birthday. Eat some hotcakes," she says as she sits back down at the large table, holding Robert in one arm and cutting bites of hotcakes for Albert with the other hand.

After breakfast, we round up the children and load them into the wagon for Uncle George to drive to school. They all wave and shout birthday wishes to me as they depart. I smile and wave back to them as they disappear around the bend. This is starting off to be a wonderful day. I am deeply blessed.

Upon entering the house, Aunt Elizabeth asks, "Ellen, can you please watch Albert and Robert and get the breakfast dishes washed? I have to go outside and take care of something."

"Sure," I reply, wondering what in the world she has to take care of outside. We don't have many chores outside except for the wash, the garden, and the chickens. The wash was completed yesterday, the garden is planted and doesn't need any tending right now, and I can't imagine what she would be doing in the chicken coop.

I place the toddlers in the middle of the floor, give them some toys to play with, and start on the dishes. As I'm washing the last plate, I hear Aunt Elizabeth enter the back door so I turn to look. I almost drop her good plate when I see her entering the house with a bloody chicken with no head in one hand, and a big butcher knife in the other. I don't think I've ever seen a woman kill a chicken before. Not that women can't do it; I've just never seen it.

"What's that for?" I ask, my nose wrinkled.

"It's for your birthday supper," she replies, as I quickly move out of the way for her to plop the bird down onto the counter.

"My birthday supper?"

"Yes, my dear girl. If I remember correctly, your favorite supper is chicken and dumplings. So, what else would we have on your special day?" She begins to yank feathers off the bird.

"Aunt Elizabeth, how do you remember that?"

"Honey, every Sunday since the day your momma married your daddy, your momma made chicken. And on your birthday, she always made chicken and dumplings because she said if she didn't, you would whine the rest of the night." She laughs.

"Sunday chicken," I mumble to myself, fondly remembering those days. "You know, I didn't realize until I was thirteen years old that Sunday was called just Sunday. We had chicken every Sunday, so I always thought it was Thursday, Friday, Saturday, Sundaychicken."

"Sundaychicken," Albert mumbles. We both look down at him. He grins up at us and says it again.

Aunt Elizabeth starts to giggle, but then she's laughing so hard, she has to stop working on the bird so she can wipe the tears from her eyes. Her laughter is contagious and soon we're both doubled over, tears running down our faces. The boys stare at us like we're crazy, which makes us laugh even harder. I try to catch my breath, but the more we try to compose ourselves, the more we can't stop laughing.

When our giggles finally subside, I say, "I can't remember the last time I laughed that hard. Thank you for letting me stay here with you, Aunt Elizabeth."

She stops working on the bird and looks deeply into my eyes. "I am so happy you are here. You don't ever need to thank me. As long as there is breath in my body, you are always welcome here."

She cuts up the chicken and places it in a cast-iron pot. "I have two surprises for you tonight."

"Surprises?"

"The first surprise is that we're having company for supper tonight. I invited the Carrington family, who lives down the road. I don't think you've met them. Peter and Ina Carrington and their family?" She cuts up an onion and places it into the pot.

I shake my head. I have not met the Carrington family. I haven't met much of anyone. I focus my time on helping Aunt Elizabeth with the house and the children. That leaves little time for much else. I say, "I don't understand. What's the surprise?"

"They're bringing their daughter and sons." She pauses and waits for me to ask.

"Sons? Plural?"

"Yes, they have five."

"And which one of these sons are you trying to fix me up with?"

She grins. "Milton. He's twenty-one years old and very handsome. Child, you are nineteen today. You can't spend the rest of your life here taking care of my children when you should be having children of your own. You're going to become an old maid if you're not careful. It's time you start thinking about your future.

Supper with the Carrington family is pleasant and relaxed. They're all friendly and talkative and I feel like I have known them forever. Aunt Elizabeth was right; Milton is very handsome. He's over six feet tall, with broad shoulders, dark hair and dark eyes that display a twinkle of mischief. He's dressed in a crisp white shirt and dark vest, but he doesn't have the top button of his shirt fastened. I don't know why, but I find his lack of properness intriguing. He has an easygoing streak with a dash of rebel in him, and I'm intoxicated by the combination.

Throughout supper, I glance over at him and he repeatedly catches me. A self-confident grin comes to his lips whenever our eyes meet, and I feel myself blushing under the scrutiny of his sparkling brown eyes. His mother catches us looking at each other and smiles, though I am so embarrassed, I wish I could crawl under the table and die.

Mrs. Carrington asks, "So, how long have you been here, Ellen?"

"It's been about five years, Mrs. Carrington."

"Are you planning on staying longer?"

I find the question a little awkward due to the fact I have nowhere else to go, but I realize she doesn't know anything about my past, so I answer in the simplest way possible. I glance at my aunt as I say, "Yes, ma'am, I live here with my aunt."

"Well, that's just wonderful. I hope we will see you on many occasions." She looks at Milton, blatant in her intentions.

Milton lifts his eyebrows at me and nods.

I shyly smile at him then look down at my plate.

Mrs. Carrington continues, "Elizabeth, this supper is just wonderful. Have you taught Ellen to make chicken and dumplings? Milton seems to be gobbling it up."

Aunt Elizabeth and I glance at each other.

"Yes, chicken and dumplings is her favorite meal."

My aunt and I giggle. I'm sure Mrs. Carrington thinks my aunt means it's my favorite meal to cook.

When supper is over, the Carringtons bid us a

good evening, and Milton and I exchange a fiery glance. His charming boyish grin tells me he will return without his family in tow, and it will be very soon. Milton exudes an air of confidence I have never seen. I'm sure he's the kind of boy who gets everything he wants the moment he wants it, and I hope I'm one of the objects he desires.

After they leave, Uncle George sits on the porch and smokes his pipe. Aunt Elizabeth and I put the children to bed and then meet in the kitchen to wash the dishes. As I wash and she dries, she asks the inevitable question. "So, what did you think of Milton? He likes you. I can tell."

"You were right—he is very handsome."

"That's it? He's handsome? But do you like him?" she asks as she takes a dripping plate from my hand.

"Sure, I guess. What's not to like? He's charming and good-looking." I reach for the cups.

"Then what?" She stops moving and looks at me, waiting for an answer.

"Well, what would a boy like that see in a girl like me?" I mumble as I keep my eyes on the cup I'm washing.

She places the half-dried plate on the counter and walks away. I wonder where she's going, but am more concerned with trying to stop myself from shedding any tears. She returns a moment later carrying a small bag.

"Here's your second surprise. I got you a birthday gift. Open it." She hands the bag to me.

I dry my hands and take the bag from her. I open the top and look inside. It contains a blue ribbon, a white ribbon, and a boar-bristle hairbrush with a beautifully carved wooden handle. I pull the brush from the bag and admire the lovely craftsmanship. I give her a hug and thank her.

"Come on." She takes me by the hand and leads me into her bedroom. She sits me down in front of her dressing table and turns me toward the mirror. She unbraids my hair and starts brushing it with my new hairbrush.

"Why do you think you are so unattractive? You've never said those exact words, but I can see it in your face and hear it in your voice," she asks.

I pause for a moment as I watch her in the mirror, brushing my dark locks. "It's just that my sisters are both pretty blondes, and so was my mother. Sometimes, I don't really feel like I fit in."

She continues brushing and doesn't say anything. After a moment of uncomfortable silence, I continue, "Daddy said that my grandma Betsy was also a pretty blonde. I'm surrounded by beautiful blonde women, and I just don't know where I got this dark hair from." I try to sound matter-of-fact, like I'm talking about the color of a mare.

Aunt Elizabeth continues to brush my hair with her right hand, and smooth it down with her left. She looks at me in the mirror. "Why would you want to look like the Carpenters?"

I don't understand the question, so I remain silent and look at her in the mirror.

When she doesn't receive a response, she continues, "Your grandma Betsy was a Carpenter. All of the Carpenters had blonde hair and blue eyes. Yes, they were beautiful, but you, my dear child, are a Rodgers. Your father was a Rodgers. Your aunt Mary is a Rodgers. I am a Rodgers. Do you think we are all unattractive?" she teases.

"No, of course not, Aunt Elizabeth. I didn't mean anything by—"

"Ellen, you are more a Rodgers than you will ever know. As a matter of fact, your daddy and I are named after our Rodgers grandparents. And so are you."

"I thought I was named after Aunt Martha Jane." I wrinkle my forehead in confusion.

"Well, maybe the Martha part of your name came from her, but the Ellen part of your name came from Elly Hays."

"I don't know who Elly Hays is. I've never heard that name before." I watch her in the mirror, hoping she'll elaborate.

"You've never heard that name?" She sounds surprised.

I shake my head.

"Elly Hays was your daddy's grandma, your great-grandma. Her full name was Elizabeth Hays, and she married James Rodgers in Tennessee when she was sixteen years old. They packed up their children and moved here to Alabama about 1811. It wasn't Alabama then; it was the Mississippi Territory. The story goes that the Creek Indians were fighting with each other and with the government, and were not happy with the Rodgers family moving onto their land. The hostile Indians stole their livestock and taunted them for years. The final straw was when the Indians burned down their house. They barely escaped with their lives."

"What happened?"

"Well, they loaded up the children and headed to Mississippi. That's how we ended up there."

I listen intently to her story. I never heard any family stories before, and I guess I never really thought about how or why my family lived in Mississippi.

"Elly Hays was a strong and brave woman. She's where I got my name, and her husband James Rodgers is where your daddy got his name. I can't believe your daddy didn't tell you stories about Grandma Elly."

I shake my head again and hope she'll continue.

"Your daddy was born en route to Mississippi, and Grandma Elly protected him with her life. As he grew, he wouldn't leave her side for one second. He loved her more than anything in the whole world and she loved him just as much. When Grandpa James died in 1826—let's see, your daddy must have been about eight years old—Grandma Elly moved away to live with one of her daughters, and your daddy was crushed. He missed her so much." She pauses. "Grandma Elly had dark hair and brown eyes, and years later when you were born with your beautiful dark hair and brown eyes, your daddy named you after the one person he loved more than anyone—Elly Hays Rodgers."

"Why didn't Aunt Mary tell me any of this when I lived with her?"

"Aunt Mary was only two years old when Grandma Elly moved away. She didn't grow up with Elly the way your daddy did. I wasn't even born yet, so I didn't know her at all. I don't know if you even remember any of this, but right after your parents died and you moved in with your aunt Mary, your grandpa Hays died." She waits for me to confirm if I remember.

I nod. "Yes, I remember when Grandpa Hays died. It must have been only a month or so after Daddy and Momma died."

"That's right. Then it wasn't more than a few weeks after that when Aunt Mary found out her husband was killed in the war. And within the next couple months, baby Monroe died, and then our mother died. I know that was a hard time for her, so I'm sure she couldn't have been thinking clearly enough to sit around the supper table filling you with great family stories. She was probably just trying to get through each day. I thought about going there to help a million times, but your uncle George was also off fighting in the war, and I was home with four babies."

"I didn't know Uncle George fought in the war."

"Yes, he was away at that time, too. A woman just can't put four babies in a wagon and travel across the country alone, especially in the middle of a war." She pauses and furrows her brow, like it's a painful memory for her.

"I remember when all of that happened, but I didn't realize those deaths were so close together. I was only nine," I mumble.

"Thank goodness you were young. It was a terrible time. I will tell you, the only way any of us survived it is because we are Rodgers." She stands up a little taller and takes a breath. I watch her face as it transforms from pain to pride.

As I try to comprehend all she has told me, she braids my hair, twists the blue and white ribbons together, and ties them at the bottom of the braid. I watch her in the mirror.

When she finishes the braid, she begins again.

"So, the moral of the story is that you are a Rodgers through and through. You are strong and beautiful just like Elly Hays Rodgers. And you are not blonde. You are worthy of a handsome boy like Milton, and probably one even better than him, but we don't have a whole bunch around here to choose from. So, Miss Ellen Rodgers, what do you think of him?"

I smile at her in the mirror. "I like him."

Milton Carrington

As I come around the bend, I see Milton sitting on the front porch, his eyes closed, chewing on a long piece of grass, his chair resting on its back two legs, leaning against the house. When he hears the wagon approach, he opens his eyes and looks toward me. He is devastatingly handsome with his shaggy hair and deep tan. He stands up and watches as I approach, a smile playing on his lips.

"Well, hello, Milton, what brings you by?" I ask. I pull back on the reins and bring the wagon to a halt in front of the porch.

He steps off the porch and offers his hand to help me down. "It has been almost a month since I've called on you, and I came to offer my apologies. I have been neglectful of a beautiful woman. Please forgive me." He looks hopeful, awaiting my reply.

I feel my knees turn to jelly and my cheeks blush. I quickly lower my eyes so he can't read the passion hidden there.

"Of course I accept your apology, but I was beginning to think I would never see you again."

"Oh, I had every intention of calling on you, but the farm has been busy."

I step up onto the porch as he speaks, and gently but firmly pull my hand from his as I stop and face him.

"My mother has asked about you on occasion, and I knew I needed to call on you so I could give her a proper report," he continues.

I don't really know what to say to him or how to act. I've never had a boy interested in me before. I've certainly never had a boy call on me. I try to avoid his stare as I stand there like an old mule. I wish Aunt Elizabeth was here to help me.

"Where are your aunt and uncle?"

"Uncle George had to take some hogs into town, and Aunt Elizabeth accompanied him to visit her doctor. She's pregnant again. They took the little ones with them, so I'm minding the older children until they return tomorrow." I quickly realize I've given him much more information than is appropriate.

"So, you're home all alone until tomorrow?" He smiles a devilish grin.

"Um, yes, but I have plenty to keep me busy with the children and the farm." I start to step toward the door but then stop, thinking it's highly improper to invite him in.

"Do you have something to drink?" he asks.

"Sure, we have some fresh buttermilk, or I could make some coffee."

"Coffee sounds great. May I walk you inside?" He offers his arm.

I reluctantly take it. "Well, all right. I guess coffee would be nice." We enter the house, without a chaperone.

We make ourselves comfortable at the table, and as we sip our coffee, we chat about his family and farm, but his deep brown eyes make it hard for me to concentrate on anything he's saying. We chat about his siblings and his hopes for the future. He even mentions that he might like to go to a big city someday, which brings up his desire to ride a train. I would tell him of my dreams of riding a train also, but I can't seem to get a word in edgewise. Throughout the one-sided conversation, he's very friendly and open, and I think I may like him a lot more than my first impression, especially his penetrating gaze. Nothing else in the world exists while I'm under that gaze.

Hours later, in the middle of a sentence, he suddenly stops and pulls out his pocket watch. "Oh, it's getting late." He rises from the table. "I need to get back to the farm, and you probably need to pick the children up from school."

Reality hits me like a lightning bolt. I hadn't thought about the time since we sat down. "Yes!" I jump up from the table. "What time is it?"

"It's almost three."

"I do have to go get the children right now. I only have a few minutes to get there. Please excuse me, Milton. It's been nice spending the afternoon with you, but I really must hurry." In one move, I grab my bonnet and head toward the door, hoping he'll hurry behind me, but he seems to be taking his time. I stand with my back against the open door, ready to close it the moment he exits.

As he nears the door, I impatiently wait for him to walk through, but he stops an inch from my face. I think he may kiss me and I feel panic rise in my chest and can't breathe. I close my eyes for a moment, but then think maybe I shouldn't because it'll look like I want him to kiss me, so I quickly open them. His full lips, that cocky grin, and those dimples are enough to set a girl's head spinning. I'm late to pick up the children, but for that split second with his mouth an inch from mine, I really would like him to kiss me. But then I get this uncomfortable feeling that spending this afternoon with him has been highly inappropriate, so I sidestep away from him and move outside onto the porch.

"Thank you for coming by, Milton. It was very nice seeing you, but I really have to run."

He steps out onto the porch, with his head cocked to one side, looking at me through squinted eyes. The afternoon sun in his face shows the slightest beginnings of lines around his eyes, and I think as he ages, he'll become more and more handsome. He shrugs and his smile widens. His smile is filled with a knowledge and confidence that's alluring, but it also unnerves me in a way I can't explain. I wish I was more attractive, more assured of myself, more experienced with boys.

I slide behind him, pull the door closed, then quickly move around him again to step off the porch. He watches me with the look of a lion stalking his prey as I climb onto the wagon.

"The visit was my pleasure, Miss Ellen, my pleasure," he says as he strolls over and places his hands on the worn wood of the wagon.

"I really do have to go now. Please come by again anytime," I mumble. Did I really just say that? Did I just invite him over again?

"Oh, I'll be back. You can count on that." He winks and his eyes twinkle.

I snap the reins and coax the horse away from

the house. I take off so fast, I almost rip Milton's hands off, but I refuse to look back and check. I know he's standing there watching me. I will not look back. I will not. No.

As I reach the bend in the road, I glance back. Sure enough, he is still standing in the yard with his arms folded across his chest, watching me and smiling. And now he knows I looked back. Oh, what a mess.

Second Date

I hear Aunt Elizabeth and Uncle George pull up in the big wagon and run out to greet them. I really need to tell my aunt what happened yesterday with Milton and ask her advice.

I think back to my sister and cousins flirting with boys at Virginia's wedding, but I wouldn't know how to flirt if someone paid to do so. It seems if a girl flirts, she's just asking for trouble, especially if there is no chaperone present.

After I tell my aunt everything that happened, she giggles and nods.

"You did exactly the right thing."

"How did I do that when I don't know what I'm doing?"

"You have to keep a man at arm's length. It sounds like he was going to try to kiss you at the door and you stopped him. He probably thinks you're playing hard to get, so now he'll be even more interested in pursuing you."

"I don't understand what you're saying. I just thought it would be improper to allow him to kiss me, so I stepped out of the way."

"Yes, it would have been improper, but that

doesn't mean a boy won't try anyway. The next time he comes around, do exactly the same thing. Keep him at a distance, and before you know it, he will bend down on one knee and propose marriage to you. *Then* you can let him kiss you." She smiles like a confident woman who knows how to tame a man.

I wish I had her poise, but at least I know what to do now…I think. And that's a good thing, because I know as sure as I'm breathing, I will be seeing Milton again very soon.

Not more than a few days later, I hear a knock at the door, and when I open it, he's grinning down at me. He has his left hand against the doorframe, his right toying with a piece of grass he's chewing. My breath is immediately taken away. I try to compose myself, but I'm sure I look foolish.

"Hello, Milton. It's nice to see you again." I run my hand through my hair, hoping I don't look like an overworked milkmaid.

He watches me for a moment. By his grin and raised eyebrow, I think he likes seeing my fingers in my hair. I do it again to see if it elicits the same response. It does.

"Hello, yourself. I'm here to invite you on a picnic."

"A picnic?"

"Yes. I would like to take you down by the river for a leisurely lunch." He gestures toward the sky. "The weather is perfect, not a cloud in the sky, so I got to thinking it would be a nice day to sit by the river and enjoy the company of a beautiful woman."

Aunt Elizabeth hears the conversation from the other room and immediately appears behind me. "Good afternoon, Milton. How is your mother?"

Milton stands up straight and clears his throat. "She is well, Mrs. Graham. How are you this fine day?"

"I am well, thank you. Is there something we can do for you?" I look back and forth between my aunt and my suitor, wondering if they have forgotten I'm standing between them.

"I came by to invite your niece on a picnic. It's a pleasant day and the river bank would be a fine place to enjoy lunch."

Aunt Elizabeth turns to me. "Ellen, I can finish everything here if you would like to join Milton for a little while."

"Um, well, all right, I guess. Let me get my bonnet."

I excuse myself as I wiggle between them. When I reach my bedroom door, I turn around and glance at them. Milton attempts to step inside, but Aunt Elizabeth doesn't move. She stands in the doorway, blocking his entrance. When I return with my bonnet, Milton holds out his arm for me, so I slip my hand in the crook and allow him to escort me to his wagon. As we drive off, my aunt waves goodbye.

Our ride has moments of awkward silence, but we manage to make some small talk. He chats about some farm owners as we pass their farms, and about the crops and rainfall. I don't really know what to say, so I just nod a lot. He talks about the nice weather we're having today, and asks if I've been down to the river yet. I shake my head. He proceeds to tell me all about the different fish he catches and goes on and on about how much I'll love it there.

After a short journey, we arrive at a beautiful glen, and through the trees spreading their branches across the banks, I can see the sparkling diamonds of the river. He's right; it is beautiful here. Weeping willow trees stand on both sides, with their lowest branches tickling the top of the water. Among them are tall, spindly pines and fragrant magnolias.

Milton grabs a quilt from the back and helps me down from the wagon. We walk arm in arm down to the water, and I watch him spread the quilt out on the ground in the clearing. He motions for me to have a seat, then returns to the wagon to retrieve the picnic basket. The moment he returns, we see a fish jump in the river. That prompts him to tell me again about how good the fishing is here.

The scenery reminds me of our creek back home. I'm suddenly melancholy and nostalgic, thinking of the times my siblings and I spent at our creek. Whatever happened to those days? I miss them—the days and my siblings. I wonder if Allen John and Willie have rivers like this in Texas.

Milton opens our picnic lunch and eyes me closely. "Has something made you sad?" he asks, looking concerned.

I'm surprised by his sincerity. "No, not sad, just remembering another place."

"Tell me about it."

I suddenly feel uncomfortable and self-conscious. I didn't notice until this very moment that we always talk about him. This is the first time he has shown interest in anything about me. What if he finds what I have to say boring? I think I should keep it short and simple.

"Oh, it's nothing. This place just looks a lot like the creek I used to live by."

"Where was that? I don't even know where

you're from."

"I used to live in Pine Springs, Mississippi."

"How did you end up here with your aunt?"

"That's a long story."

"I have time." He smiles and lies back, leaning on his elbows.

"Well, my parents both died when I was nine."

"That's terrible. I didn't know." He rolls over on his side to face me, leaning on one arm while reaching over to pick a long piece of grass. He places it in his mouth, and I completely lose my train of thought. He smiles again when he notices me looking at his mouth. I blush and look down.

"Yes, it was terrible, but I was taken in by my aunt Mary. She's my aunt Elizabeth's sister."

"How did you end up here?"

"We lost so many family members to illness and the war, and the place was too depressing after that. I just had to get out of there, and the only place I had to go was here, so here I am."

"That's so sad. I'm very sorry about your parents, but I'm glad you're here."

Observing the look of concern on his face, I am convinced Milton is the most amazing person I have ever met. He turns to the river, and I watch his lips caress the blade of grass, wondering if he likes me as much as I like him, and find myself wishing he would kiss me.

"I think you belong here. I might even think you belong right here with me." He looks at me through his long lashes, and I can feel my cheeks getting hot. He lies down all the way, resting the side of his head on his hand.

"Did you have a boyfriend in Mississippi?"

I shake my head.

"Have you ever kissed a boy?"

I shake my head again.

He grins. "Well, I won't rush you. When you are ready for a kiss, you let me know." The caring man I witnessed moments ago suddenly transforms into the cocky boy I first met. He lies there like he's expecting me to beg him to kiss me right now. I will not give him the pleasure. If he wasn't so handsome, I would be infuriated by his lack of manners. I have a feeling we're playing a weird cat-and-mouse game, and since I'm not experienced enough with boys to be sure, I just turn away and gaze at the river.

"I think you'd like me to kiss you right now."

I look at him. "Not if I have to ask you."

"You don't have to. I just thought it would be more gentlemanly of me to allow you to ask first."

I watch him lick his lips. They beckon me. I rise on my hands and knees and move toward him, stopping an inch from his face. "You may kiss me if you wish."

He stares into my eyes and touches my hair. "I would like that very much." The sweet boy has returned. The look in his eyes is intoxicating. This is it. This is what I've been looking for.

He inches forward and touches his lips to mine. His lips are soft and warm. I close my eyes and allow them to take mine.

When I return home, Aunt Elizabeth is bubbling with excitement. "How did it go? Do you really like him? He likes you. What did you talk about? Are you going to see him again?"

She won't stop talking long enough for me to give her any details. My heart is fluttering and I can't get the smile off my face. I think I'm in love. I also think I am frustrated by his cockiness. His confidence is attractive; the fact that he knows it is not.

"Yes, I really like him," is all I can squeeze in.

"I knew it!" she says, as she runs out of the room to get one of the children who is whining about something.

I open the front door to feel the afternoon sun on my face. I lean against the doorframe with my eyes closed and tilt my face toward the warmth, wishing Milton would turn around and come back. I can't wait until the next time I see him. I will allow him to kiss me again.

July 1874

"It's so nice to meet you," the blonde says. "Milton has told us all about you."

"Thank you. It's nice to meet you also, um…I'm sorry, I don't know your name." I feel my face flush with embarrassment.

"Sue. My name is Sue. I've known Miltie my whole life. We all have." She waves her hand around at all the young adults milling around at the barbecue.

The name sounds familiar, and she looks familiar, too.

"Yes, welcome. It's nice to meet you," another girl says as she approaches us. "I'm Bethany." She reaches to shake my hand.

Oh, my goodness, they're the girls from church. They don't recognize me, and I haven't seen them in, what? Six years?

Bethany continues without skipping a beat. "I live right down the road from Miltie."

"You all call him Miltie?" I ask.

"Sure, don't you?" Sue says.

"Um, well, no. I guess I never thought about it."

"Wait. Haven't you two been dating for a long time?" Sue asks. Bethany also looks a little surprised.

"Yes, I guess we have. Almost two years."

"Did he try to kiss you right away? He kisses all the girls right—" She stops abruptly. "I'm sorry, that wasn't what I meant to say. Please excuse me. I see someone I need to say hello to." Sue scampers off, waving at some newcomers.

At that very moment, Milton walks up and nods hello to Bethany, who also quickly excuses herself and flees across the lawn. I watch as she glances back over her shoulder and bats her eyes at Milton. When she notices me watching her, she turns away and walks even faster.

Milton smiles and hands me a cup of cool cider. "I see you met Sue and Bethany."

"Yes. Have you known them long?"

"Sure, my whole life. All of these people are neighbors. I can't believe you don't already know them all."

"Well, I spend most of my time helping my aunt with the children, so I don't get out much, unless I'm with you, and you have never taken me to a social gathering before." I take a sip of my cider and wonder why we haven't gone to any functions. I also wonder about the girls he kisses right away. "Why is that, Milton?"

"Why is what?" he asks as he waves and nods to some people.

"Why haven't you taken me to any social gatherings with your friends before?"

"I guess it just never came up." He shrugs as he sips his cider, looking around at everyone.

"Are any of these girls old flames of yours?"

He looks at me with confusion. "What do you mean?"

"It's a simple question, Milton. Have you ever dated any of these girls?"

He sighs. "Listen, I've never been out of this town, so who do you think I've been dating? Of course I have. I've probably dated most of them at one time or another. Why are you asking me that?" His cool, confident demeanor has vanished.

"I just never thought that I would look like the next girl in line for you, that's all. I guess I never considered that you dated someone else before."

I don't know why jealousy is rearing its ugly head. I try to think rationally. Milton is a good-looking man, and he is certainly not a child. Of course he dated other girls before me.

"That was before you and I started dating, right?"

"Well, mostly. I mean, you and I aren't married or anything." He shrugs again and sips his cider as he eyes a girl walking by.

Anger surges through my body, like someone has lit a fire under the very spot where I'm standing. I thrust my cup into his chest, turn, and march toward the road.

"Wait, Ellen! Where are you going? Let me walk with you," he says as he follows me, a cup in each hand and cider dripping down the front of his white shirt.

I don't respond. I keep walking. I don't want to hear any of his excuses, and I certainly don't want to stand here amongst the girls he has been dating behind my back and look like a fool.

After a few minutes of chasing me and getting no response, Milton finally gives up and heads back to the party. I continue to walk alone. I wish I could cry, but all I feel is anger. At Milton, at myself. How could I have been so dumb to think a boy like that would ever care for a girl like me?

I walk for a couple of hours, and realize I don't know how far away from home I am. The orange sunset fades, turning the sky to black. With every little snap of a twig in the woods, and every scurry of a nighttime creature, I'm feeling more and more anxious. I jump at each little sound in the trees around me. I pick up my pace and pray I make it home in one piece. So many shadows and noises make me feel like the woods are closing in. My anger dissipates as fear fills my mind, and by the time I turn the bend and see the house, I'm nearly in a full run.

It's such a relief to see Aunt Elizabeth sitting on the front porch. She has a quilt wrapped around her and she stands as I come into view.

"Thank goodness you are home. It's late and I was worried about you. Why are you walking? Where is Milton?" She wants to talk. She wants answers. I just want to cry. I wrap my arms around her pregnant waist, bury my head into her quilt, and sob.

When my crying finally subsides, I tell her the whole story.

A New Beginning

After a restless night, I feel even worse in the morning. Every muscle in my body is sore from the long walk, and I'm embarrassed by the situation I find myself in. I was positive Milton had feelings for me. I was sure he loved me. I thought he would come for me last night, but he didn't. Now I feel even more like a fool.

After breakfast, we send the children off to school, and I begin my daily chores by washing the dishes. As I stand at the counter, Aunt Elizabeth comes to help me dry and says, "I have to admit, I wondered why he hadn't proposed already. I mean, you two have been together for what, two years now?" She grimaces, reaches down, and absentmindedly rubs her pregnant belly. "I think you should either ask him directly what his intentions are or refuse to see him completely."

Of course she knows best. She's an experienced and mature woman who has been married fifteen years and birthed eight children, with another on the way.

"Refuse to see him is what I would like to do, but I really care for him. It just hurts. I never thought he was seeing other girls. I assumed when he wasn't with me, he was working on his daddy's farm. I should have known a boy like that would never truly be interested in me." I pout, but refuse to cry any more tears over him.

"Nonsense. You just need to ask his intentions flat out."

As we finish the last of the dishes, a knock comes on the door, and I know it's him. Aunt Elizabeth excuses herself, picks up one-year-old Oscar, and takes him into her bedroom. I slowly open the front door and look up at him without saying a word.

"I'm sorry," he says.

"No need to be," I reply, trying to sound nonchalant and hoping my puffy eyes don't give me away.

"Can we go somewhere and talk?"

"I don't really know what there is to say, Milton."

"Please." His sad brown eyes resemble that of a puppy in pain, and I feel a combination of wanting to wrap my arms around him and slam the door in his face. "Let's go down to the river. You like it there." He smiles as he takes my hand. I allow him to lead me toward his wagon.

The ride to the river is painfully silent. I don't know where to start, and apparently, he doesn't, either. When we arrive, he pulls the quilt out of the back and spreads it on the grass. I reluctantly sit down and he sits next to me. Could anything be more uncomfortable than this?

He takes my hands in his. "Please tell me what made you so upset yesterday."

I look at him for a moment, not understanding how he couldn't know why I am upset. I'm torn between being truthful, as Aunt Elizabeth advised, and screaming at him for his ignorance. I decide there will be no games.

"I didn't realize you were seeing other girls, and I feel you made me look like a fool."

I wait for him to respond.

"I haven't really been seeing anyone else, not seriously, anyway. And besides, I didn't know you and I were having a serious relationship. Do you want more from me?"

I'm almost tempted to slap him and walk home again. What does he think I want after two years? I sigh. "Yes, I want more. I thought I already had more. I thought we were heading toward marriage, family, you know, the logical thing. I'm twenty-one years old, and as of yesterday, it's obvious to me that I am no closer to having my own family now than I ever was. Am I wasting my time, Milton?"

"I didn't realize you wanted those things." He looks down at our hands entwined. "Are you waiting for a marriage proposal?"

Now what do I say? Yes would be the truthful answer, but if he's cavorting with other women, then no. I'm so confused.

"By your lack of response, I would guess the answer is yes, but I'm sorry, I can't do that right now. I work for my daddy. I don't have a way to support a wife and a family. Maybe someday my daddy will give me some land and then we can make it work. But for now, I just don't see it." He looks deeply into my eyes and awaits a response. The look I see is not quite the look of love I long for.

"So, we are never going to get married," I say.

"I wouldn't say never. I just think it will be a little

while longer, that's all."

I pull my eyes from his and look out at the river, questioning if this whole relationship is only in my head, and wondering what I should do now. He reaches over, puts his finger under my chin, and turns my face back to him. "Will you wait for me?"

I meet his eyes. He is so sad and forlorn. My heart melts at his touch and tender question. How can I say no to this man? He's simply waiting for the time to be right. I have trusted him until now. A woman cannot expect a man to remain faithful if she's not married to him. There has been no vow. I have been stupid for causing such a ruckus because of my jealousy.

I nod and a tear rolls down my cheek. He wipes it away with his thumb as he leans over and kisses me softly on the lips. I hope everything will turn out all right.

September 1875

"The doctor said your aunt has developed pneumonia. She can't get out of bed," Uncle George says to me as he sits at the breakfast table, watching Cornelia give baby Dora a bottle. "She's burning up with fever and isn't responding to anything the doctor is giving her. Loucinda is going to stay with her again today."

I'm not surprised Aunt Elizabeth is getting worse. For the last few years, I've watched her health fail more and more. "Why isn't anyone else in the house sick?" I ask, sitting down at the table with my cup of coffee.

"I don't know. I don't know how or when it started or why we're not sick, too. I have to run into town for a few hours. Will you be all right with the children again today? Cornelia will stay home from school to help you." Uncle George doesn't wait for an answer. He rises, pours himself half a cup of coffee, and stands at the counter drinking it.

He turns back to me and shrugs. "I don't know what else we can do, except what the doctor says. He says we need to pray."

He finishes the last gulp of his coffee and puts the cup on the counter. I watch as he heads out the back door to go to work.

I rise to close the door behind him and stop to look out at the horizon. Gazing across the field, I wonder if we're going to lose Aunt Elizabeth. She has been in bed for a week now, and has grown even paler and thinner. She looked awful after she had Oscar, then immediately got pregnant with Dora. After Dora's birth, it took her two months to recover enough just to crawl out of bed.

I don't understand why she's growing weaker. I think it started as something sick inside of her, and now it's pneumonia. I don't think she's going to get better this time, and the thought makes me nauseous.

I shake my head, trying to make the thought go away. I can't bear the thought of living without her. The last serious illness I witnessed was my parents', but the fever they had was highly contagious and many people caught it and died. One would think the doctors could cure pneumonia. If they know what it is, why can't they fix it?

I close the door and wash the breakfast dishes. Since Cornelia is staying home today, I decide I will ride over to Milton's house and speak with his mother. I know the doctor is a smart man and Aunt Loucinda is here to help, but I can't imagine talking to another person will do any harm. It might actually do some good. And truthfully, I want to see Milton. My heart is so heavy for my aunt, and I want to feel Milton's arms around me, reassuring me everything will be all right.

I poke my head into the bedroom and whisper to Aunt Loucinda that I'll return in an hour. I glance at Aunt Elizabeth. Her breathing is labored and has a rattle to it. She's as white as the pillow she's lying on, and is dreadfully thin. I hate to think it, but she looks like she's dead already. I close the door, stifle a sob, and head to Milton's.

Milton's mother isn't much help. She offers to make a pot of stew to send over for the family and that's about all I can get out of her. I thank her for her kindness, though I'm very disappointed she has no idea what to do.

"I really need to get back home, but I would like to see Milton first. Is he here?" I ask.

"Yes, he's around here somewhere. Why don't you check the barn, and if you don't see him around there, check down by the river. He mentioned something about going there for something."

"Thank you, Mrs. Carrington. I'll see you again soon."

"You're welcome, Ellen. I hope your aunt gets better quickly."

I nod and gently close the front door on my way out.

I walk back to the barn, calling Milton's name, but receive no answer, and I don't see anyone else, either, so I walk back to my horse and ride down to the river.

When I arrive, I find Milton's wagon in its usual place, and I wonder what in the world he's working on down here.

I tie my horse to the back of his wagon and walk into the familiar clearing where we have spent many romantic hours. I freeze in my tracks, as I see Milton lying on the blanket on the ground, kissing a girl!

How can he do this to me? *Again?* I thought we were to be married. I thought he loved me.

They didn't hear me approach, but as my eyes fill

with tears, a whimper escapes my throat, and they both jump. Milton and the girl both face me. It's the girl from the barbecue, the one from church. What is her name? Sue! I can't believe it.

I turn away and try to think of a logical reason for what I witnessed, but I know there is none. I lift my skirt, run back to my horse, and fumble through my tears to untie the lead. I climb up, not taking care to adjust my skirt, snap the reins, and ride off as fast as I can. I don't even know where I'm going. All I know is I have to get away from here.

I vaguely wish Milton would follow me and offer a reason and apology, but I know he can't explain what I saw. The only explanation is, he's a skirt chaser and I'm a fool. After a while, I pull back on the reins and allow the horse to slow to a walk. I look behind me, but Milton is not there. Part of me is angry that he didn't follow, and part of me is glad, because I never want to see him again. I slowly walk the horse back home.

I ride up to the house, my face covered in streaks from tears mixed with dirt from the dusty road. Aunt Loucinda and Uncle George are sitting on the porch. As I climb down, I can tell something is terribly wrong. Both of their faces are tearstained, their shoulders are slumped.

"What's wrong?" I ask them.

Aunt Loucinda says flatly, "Your aunt is dead."

"What? I just left and she was…no, she can't be!"

"She's gone, Ellen," Uncle George confirms in a stern tone, staring at his boots.

I dash into the house, slamming the front door behind me, and run into the bedroom. Aunt

Elizabeth is lying in her bed, covered in her brown and green patchwork quilt. She looks peaceful, like she's sleeping, but her skin is even whiter than before and her lips are blue.

"No."

I approach the bed and fall down on the floor beside her. I touch her hand and quickly pull back as I find it cold.

"No."

Her chest is not moving; she's no longer struggling to breathe. I rub my hand down the side of her face and try to grasp that she's no longer hot with fever. She can't be gone, not when I need her so.

"No, no, no."

I feel like I'm going to shrivel up and blow away like dust. The only person who loves me is gone, just like my daddy, just like my momma. I can't catch my breath as I sob and lay my head down on the bed and wish I would die right here with her.

The tears flow as I feel the guilt of not saying goodbye to her. I didn't have a chance to say goodbye to my parents. I had the chance today with my aunt, but I didn't take it. My sobs turn into wails as I think of her loving eyes.

"Please open your eyes," I whisper. "Please."

She will never again open her eyes. She will never again look at me with love.

Funeral

The children and I slowly walk back to the house following the funeral. I carry baby Dora as she sleeps. Aunt Elizabeth's death has haunted my dreams for the last two nights and I'm exhausted.

In keeping with my somber mood, the sky is gray and overcast. It rained all morning and the road is filled with puddles. Albert and Robert, in typical little-boy fashion, jump in every one of them on the walk back to the house. I should request they not do that, but I don't see the point now that they're covered in mud up to their knees. They are both going to need hot baths when we get home, but I don't know where I'll get the energy to make it happen. I don't know how I will survive losing my aunt, but I need to step up and take care of these children. I run my hand over my unkempt hair and think I don't even have the energy to take care of myself.

I watch Uncle George as he shuffles in front of us, carrying two-year-old Oscar, who is sleeping on his shoulder. I wonder what Uncle George is going to do now without a wife. I assume he'll need me to stay and help with the children, but I'm not sure he wants me here. He has always been cordial with me, but I've always wondered if it was only because of my relationship with my aunt. It seems he couldn't care less about me one way or the other. I guess I'll have to find some alone time with him and ask if I should stay or leave. But if I leave, where would I go?

When we finally arrive back at the house, I warm up some okra and greens, slice the bread Aunt Loucinda brought over yesterday, and put supper on the table. Following our solemn meal, I get the children washed up and ready for bed, and when they're all tucked in for the night, I think that it's probably a good time to speak with Uncle George.

I search the entire house but can't find him. I check the front porch but he isn't there. I look out the back door toward the barn, but I don't see a lantern burning. He can't be out there in the dark. I really need to speak with him about the future, but I'm so fatigued, I give up and go to bed.

When the rooster crows, I wake the children, make them breakfast, and take them to school. When I return, I search the house and barn again, but Uncle George is still nowhere to be found. The entire day goes by and he doesn't appear. Even when I return from picking the children up from school, I still can't find him, and begin to worry. Where in the world did he disappear to?

While I'm putting supper on the table, the children ask after his whereabouts. I tell them he had some farm business to attend to in town and will return soon. I hope I'm right. I don't know what I'll tell them if he does not reappear by nightfall to kiss them goodnight.

Fortunately, as we're eating supper, he walks in the front door and sits down at the table with us. I don't say a word about his whereabouts, and he doesn't volunteer the information. Maybe he just needed some time alone to sort out all that has happened. Maybe he went into town and got drunk and passed out somewhere last night to sleep it off. That would explain the way he looks and smells. His eyes are bloodshot, his clothes are wrinkled, and his face is dirty. After putting the children to bed, I find him on the porch, but he refuses to speak to me, so I don't push him.

As the days pass, Uncle George is absent more than he is home. I give up the idea of asking him if I should stay, because it's obvious I am needed here. The children have lost their mother, and apparently have lost their father at the same time. Milton has shown up on the porch a few times, but I don't have the energy to deal with him. Yesterday, I slammed the door right in his face. I hope he doesn't come back.

Within a few weeks, I find myself more comfortable in my role as sole caretaker for the children. John is now sixteen and does not stay home very much. If he's not helping his father on the farm, he's riding into town to see his friends. I can't blame him. If I had friends in town, I would go there, too. Cornelia is now fifteen and is a huge help. She quit school when her mother died and helps every day with the younger children. But she is so terribly quiet and sad about her mother that my heart aches for her. She's dealing with her heartache alone, and will not speak with me or allow me to help her.

Laura is the one who really breaks my heart. She's nine—the same age I was when my mother died. I can't stand the thought of her feeling as sad and lonely as I did. I make every effort to spend extra time with her, but with nine children in the house, there isn't much extra time to be had.

William and Beulah pretty much take care of themselves, but Albert and Robert are handfuls, and Oscar and Dora are so little, they're about all I can handle. I carry one or both of them on my hip at all times. They're all very good children, but they're still a lot of work. After a few months, we're beginning to settle into a routine. The house is clean, food is on the table, and the children are starting to come around. They actually play and smile on occasion. When someone mentions their mother, they don't dissolve into tears and become sullen. This is a huge improvement.

Though we're starting to feel better, Uncle George is still disappearing every evening. He has begun leaving earlier and earlier, and hasn't shared supper with us in a few weeks. I wonder what he's up to.

Tonight, while the children and I are eating supper, he unexpectedly makes an appearance and introduces us to his new lady friend—Lucrecia.

March 1879

Lucrecia was only here once in a while in the beginning, but now she's here just about every day. She seems to be trying to fit into the family, but she's stepping on more than a few toes as far as the children are concerned. They are not pleased with this woman openly trying to take their momma's place. And she gives me the impression I'm not welcome here any longer, which makes me angry. This is my home, not hers. These are my cousins. However, judging by Uncle George's loving gaze, he's building a serious relationship with her.

She's only a year or so older than I, so one would think we would be the best of friends, but she acts so much younger. The word that comes to mind is immature. She never behaves badly around Uncle George or the children, but when we're alone, she rattles off snippy little comments like, "Don't you have a date this evening?" and "How long are you going to stay with your uncle instead of getting married yourself?" I know she's just being petty, but I'm tired of listening to her comments.

What can I do besides take her aside and tell her to stop? For some reason, I don't think that will go over well with Uncle George. He's very protective of her. She wants to be the lady of the house, and that's impossible with me around. She wants me gone, that's for sure, and I'm sure it's only a matter of time before she gets her way.

The children aren't very happy about her telling them to call her "Aunt Lou," which is annoying to the older ones. They mind their manners around her, but when they're sure she can't see them, I catch them rolling their eyes at each other. I refuse to discipline them for that because I would like to roll my eyes, too. They haven't said anything to me about their feelings, but I know them better than anyone.

When Uncle George and "Aunt Lou" announce their plans to marry, I collapse on my bed and cry for an hour. It's not that I'm unhappy for Uncle George; of course he deserves to be happy and I wish him the best. What makes me sad is that if Lucrecia is to be the new woman of the house and the stepmother of these children, where does that leave me? I love these children, and I'm rapidly feeling more uncertain about my future. Can I be casually discarded like an old rag? I am family, but I don't think Uncle George ever felt that way about me. I have never gotten a single thank you or a kind word of appreciation for helping him out. I've seldom even gotten a smile out of the man.

As the wedding date approaches, "Aunt Lou" makes it more and more obvious that I need to find a new place to live. Once I'm gone, she can pretend this is her family. I feel so sorry for the children, and I can't believe Uncle George is letting her get away with this. And where can I go? What can I do? I don't want to go back to Uncle Hays's house. I guess I have only one choice: I need to go back to Mississippi.

I sit down and write my little sister a letter.

My dearest Necie,

I miss you and Lizzie and would love to come to Mississippi and see you both. Uncle George has announced his plans to remarry, and I feel I will be unwelcome in the home of his new wife. Please speak with Lizzie and David, and write me as to where I can stay upon my return home. I look forward to seeing you all. If someone can find room for me to stay, I will immediately ask Uncle Hays for assistance in getting home.

Please tell Aunt Mary I said hello, and hopefully, I'll see her very soon.

Love to everyone.

Your sister,
Ellen Rodgers

As I await a return letter from Necie, the distance between me and Uncle George grows into a great chasm. Late in the evenings, when the house is quiet, I frequently hear Lucrecia behind closed doors, chastising him that he hasn't thrown me out. I know she's purposely speaking loudly for all to hear, but I'm saddened that he does not stand up for me. At the very least, he could ask her to lower her voice. He has not yet asked me to leave, but I expect it very soon. He won't make eye contact with me, and never speaks a word to me.

Finally, after weeks of waiting, I receive word back from Necie.

Dear Ellen,

It is so wonderful to hear from you, and I'm sorry you

don't feel welcome there anymore. Of course, Lizzie and I would love to have you come home and stay with us. We don't have much room here, but you are welcome anyway.

Lizzie and David discussed our sleeping arrangements, and I told him I'll share my bed with you. I will do anything to get you home. I've missed you so much and I'm so happy you are coming.

Please speak with Uncle Hays this very minute and be on your way to us.

I await your return.

I love you,
Necie Rodgers

I feel a sense of relief, and I smile at the thought of seeing my sisters again. Necie has always been a feisty little thing, and I wish she were here to put Lucrecia in her place. I giggle at the thought of Necie in her little pigtails wagging her finger in Lucrecia's face. Of course I realize Necie doesn't wear pigtails anymore.

I can't believe Lizzie and David have three children. Time is flying by. I didn't realize it, but I've been gone far too long. I'll miss my little cousins here, but the more I think about returning home, the more excited I become. Yes, home. My home. The place I grew up. Seeing the family I have neglected for so long. It's time to return. I'll ride over to speak with Uncle Hays first thing in the morning. I close my eyes, take a deep breath, and feel my shoulders relax for the first time in a very long time.

Begging for a Ride

"But, Uncle Hays, I don't know how to do it by myself. You simply have to help me go back to Mississippi." I hear myself whining like a five-year-old.

"What do you want me to do, Ellen? Drive you myself? I have a business to maintain here. I don't have time to cart you all the way back there. You're twenty-five years old. You'll have to be a grown-up for a change and figure it out yourself." He scowls. Then under his breath, he adds, "Maybe if you hadn't run that nice boy Milton off, you wouldn't be in this predicament."

"Uncle Hays, he was seeing other girls. Was I supposed to just turn a blind eye to his behavior?"

"Other women would have. He has a good farm and is very well off."

"His father has a good farm. He has nothing. Nothing but roaming eyes and loose lips." I lean against the fence post, crossing my arms over my chest, wondering what I'm supposed to do now. Finally I say, "I guess I'll have to walk, then."

I start to stomp away, disappointed and angry at the lack of help from my only family in Alabama.

"Wait," Uncle Hays says.

I stop and turn to look at him standing in the middle of his smelly, snorting hogs.

"You can't walk. Maybe I can come up with some money to hire someone to take you to Mississippi. It won't be a fancy coach, more like a broken wagon with a load of moonshine, but at least it could get you there safely, without you trying to make it on your own." He looks up at me. "You are my brother's daughter. I guess I can't let you roam around the country without an escort. I'll see what I can do. You come back tomorrow and I'll let you know." He turns and walks away.

Tears of joy and gratitude fill my eyes. "Oh, thank you, Uncle Hays," I say, but he's already out of earshot.

I return to Uncle George's and pack my meager belongings.

When Uncle George sees me in the kitchen, folding my dresses on the table, he looks confused, then relieved, then saddened.

"What are you doing?" he asks quietly, turning away and placing a cup in the washbasin. Those are the first words he has spoken to me in weeks.

"Uncle Hays is arranging an escort to take me back to Mississippi. You have Lucrecia here to help you now, so I guess I'm not really needed…or wanted here." I don't stop packing or look up at him as I speak.

"Oh, all right. When will you be leaving?" he asks as he opens the cupboard and stares into it.

"I have to go back to Uncle Hays's tomorrow

and find out the details, but I imagine it'll be very soon, maybe even tomorrow or the day after."

He doesn't say anything else, but stands with his hand on the open cupboard door, staring at the shelves.

I stop packing and turn toward him. "Is there anything else?"

After a moment's pause, he says, "She loved you very much." His voice cracks.

I feel tears coming to my eyes. "I know, and I loved her." I go back to packing, picking up the carved hairbrush my aunt gave me on my birthday. Both she and my mother, women I loved, are now gone. A tear falls onto my folded dress. I stop packing and look at it.

"I'm sorry about the way things have turned out." He still hasn't taken his eyes from the cupboard.

"Me, too." I know he's referring to the situation with Lucrecia, but I don't want to spend our last conversation discussing her. It's too little, too late. I make a feeble attempt to turn the conversation back to Aunt Elizabeth. "I wish she hadn't died."

"Yeah." He closes the cupboard door, turns away, and ever so slowly shuffles out the front door.

I stop folding my clothes and turn to watch him. His shoulders are slumped and his posture is that of a beaten man. He looks as though he has aged twenty years in the last three. Even though I've been so angry with him for not standing up for me, I suddenly feel very sorry for him. Another tear falls from my face onto my dress, a tear for him.

He closes the door behind him without looking back. I wipe my face with my palm. It doesn't matter how angry or sorry I feel, I am leaving, perhaps as soon as tomorrow. I place my dress into the bag, extinguish the lamp, go to my room, and crawl into bed.

On the day of my journey, I spend a somber morning saying goodbye to the children. Throughout breakfast, they're sullen and sad that I won't be there anymore. I know they will miss me, and God knows I'll miss them terribly. Before they leave for school, they all hug me and we shed many tears. I tell them I'll write often, and promise that when I'm settled, they're all welcome to visit me in Mississippi.

I don't speak to Lucrecia; I don't even look in her general direction. She's very quiet this morning. It's a shame that we are so close in age and yet missed the opportunity to be good friends, but what happened between us was obviously not my doing. I feel sorry for the children and Uncle George, but my heart does not go out to Lucrecia. No, "Aunt Lou" will have to make it on her own.

After I straighten up the kitchen and check my room one last time for stray belongings, I walk out the front door with my bag under my arm. I whisper a quiet and stern "Goodbye, Lucrecia."

As the door closes, I hear her say, "Goodbye, Ellen."

I stand on the porch for a moment, trying to figure out why it's so easy for me to leave here. The only conclusion I can come to is that this was Aunt Elizabeth's home, and now she's gone. Half of me wants to cry that it's over, and half of me wants to burst out in song that I am going home.

I step off the front porch and begin the long walk to Uncle Hays's house. As I pass familiar farmhouses and bends in the road, I think back to the promising life I so eagerly expected when I arrived here. I enjoyed every moment with my aunt and her children, but other than that, Alabama has not been the land of milk and honey I imagined it would be. I slowly come to the realization that I came here because I was trying to run away from something in Mississippi, and now that I have grown up, it's time to stop running. It's time to go home and face my past. It's been almost thirteen years since I've been home, but it seems like only yesterday I traveled this road to Aunt Elizabeth's house for the first time.

The closer I get to Uncle Hays's, the more I'm ready to leave. I don't care if it takes seven days or three months to get home. I pick up my pace now that I'm sure I'm doing the right thing. Yes, it's time to go home. It's time to begin my future.

Home Again

Uncle Hays did exactly as he promised. There are two covered wagons parked in front of his house, and I can't control my excitement. I hike up my skirt and run up to the house, admiring the wagons as I get closer. They look like the promise of a new day.

I slow down a bit as I get my first glimpse of the driver sitting in the front wagon. He's a little on the burly side, about fifty, and looks as if he hasn't bathed since he was forty. His clothes are faded, wrinkled, and dirty, his chin covered with gray stubble. I would bet my last dollar if he smiled, he would be missing quite a few teeth.

I nod at him and smile. He barely nods back and doesn't smile. He pulls a half-smoked cigar from his front pocket, places it between his lips, and lights it while looking at me sideways through squinted eyes. As he puffs, smoke swirls around his head, settling under the brim of his hat like a fog. When I hurry past him, I can feel him turn and watch me walk around the back of the wagon.

The driver in the second wagon is a younger man, maybe in his early twenties. He's dressed in dark pants and a vest, with a floppy brown hat that has many holes in it, as if it has been chewed on by a couple rats. Under his weathered clothes, he looks like a fairly handsome young man. He watches me with no expression at all as I pass between the two wagons. I step up onto the front porch and don't look back at him, but I can feel him also watching me as I speak with Uncle Hays.

My uncle explains to me he hired these wagons, which are headed to Vicksburg, to take me home. They will pass right through Meridian on the way. I thank Uncle Hays and give him a hug. He pats me on the back. I guess that's as close to a hug as he can give. In an unprecedented show of concern, he tells me to write him the moment I get home and let him know I arrived safely. I promise to do so, and head back down the steps to the wagons.

The boy driving the second wagon points to the first wagon. I assume he means for me to climb into that one, so I hike up my skirt, and crawl into the back of the first wagon in a very unladylike manner. I hear my uncle tell the burly driver to make sure he takes me directly to the front door of my sister's house. The driver assures him I am in good hands. He then snaps the reins, and we are off. Trying not to lose my balance, I squeeze my way between crates and barrels, and eye a pile of hay and blankets that looks like the most comfortable place to sit.

When I sit down, the blankets grunt and the hay moves. I jump back up and let out a small shriek. I almost sat on a man who was sleeping under the blankets.

"Oh, I'm very sorry," he grumbles as he sits up.

"No, no, sir, it was entirely my fault. I'm sorry for waking you."

"You must be the young lady we're taking to

Meridian." He brushes the hay off his shoulders.

"Yes, sir, my name is Ellen."

"Nice to meet you, Ellen. I'm Buck. I'm a sharpshooter, and I always go along on these trips."

"It's a pleasure to meet you." I smile and sit down on a wooden box across from him, holding my bag tightly on my lap.

I wonder what kind of trip would require the skills of a sharpshooter. I eye the stranger and tell myself he's probably only here to hunt supper for us, but my gut tells me there is something more going on that I don't want to know. I decide to not worry myself, for Uncle Hays has confidence in these men.

I try to keep my eyes focused on the second wagon out the back, but find myself stealing glances at Buck. He's quite handsome, with a strong jaw and the slightest of fine lines around his eyes. I blush as I think the next few days may be more pleasant than I first imagined. When Buck catches me looking at him, I smile sheepishly, then turn my attention out the back of the wagon again.

As we move up the road, Aunt Loucinda appears on the porch with Uncle Hays. I smile and wave at her, and as usual, she doesn't wave back. I wonder if Uncle Hays and Aunt Loucinda are sad or glad that I'm leaving. I imagine the latter. After thirteen years, it doesn't really matter.

Even though I'm a little nervous about traveling with strangers, I know Uncle Hays has paid these men good money to watch over me. With every mile, I feel myself relax, and as the horses clip-clop on the dry, dusty road, I'm soon lulled into a deep sleep by the rocking of the wagon.

When I wake, it's almost dark out. We're not

moving and I assume we have stopped for the night. I listen but don't hear the gentlemen talking of setting up tents like we did when I came here with Uncle Hays. I hear someone mumbling but can't make out what he's saying. I decide to find out what's going on. I grab the shawl from my bag, wrap it around my shoulders, and stiffly crawl down from the back of the wagon.

There are four men sitting around a large campfire eating something, and it sure does smell good.

"Well, there she is," says Buck. "Are you hungry?"

"Yes, sir, it smells delicious. Are we stopped for the night?" I ask stupidly, trying to make polite conversation. I step toward the blazing fire. The men have placed some logs around it to sit on. Buck pats the log he's sitting on, gesturing for me to sit next to him.

"Yes, we're planting ourselves right here for the night," he says. "Did you meet everyone?"

I shake my head as one of the men hands me a metal plate with some kind of meat and a piece of bread on it. I take it and sit next to Buck. I am so hungry I know I'll eat all of this, no matter what it is.

I place the plate on my lap as Buck begins the introductions, starting with the young man who was driving the second wagon.

"This is my son, Luke." Luke nods and I nod back.

Yes, I see the resemblance between the two. Luke looks just like his father, minus the wisps of gray hair and the lines around his eyes. Buck then points to the man who handed me the plate. He must have been in the back of Luke's wagon the whole time.

"This is Earl, our cook."

I nod at Earl, whose face makes him look thirtysomething because it has no wrinkles, but he has so much gray in his hair, I would swear he's older. Buck then nods toward the burly driver, who's sitting off in the shadows smoking a cigar. "And that's Floyd." Floyd nods, winks at me, and grins a toothless grin. I knew he didn't have any teeth. I nod back and smile weakly. Something about Floyd doesn't feel right. He stares at me like I'm his supper. I vow to stay as far away from this man as possible for the remainder of the trip.

Buck continues, "So, why are you headed to Meridian?"

I swallow the food I was chewing. "That's my home, although I haven't been there for almost thirteen years. I'm moving back."

"That's your uncle who hired us?" Buck asks.

"Yes, my uncle Hays. And I'm very grateful for the escort. Thank you all." I look at them one by one in the campfire light, but they don't return the smile, and none of them say, "You're welcome" or "Our pleasure." I immediately feel like the outsider that I am, and I wonder why I always end up in the company of people who don't want me around. As usual, I resign to staying quiet and out of the way for the rest of the trip.

Following our campfire supper and some polite conversation, the men lie down right where they are and go to sleep. I climb back into the wagon, though it feels a lot chillier away from the fire. I pull the blanket off the floor of the wagon, shake some hay off of it, and wrap it around my shoulders. I listen to a hoot owl as I drift off to sleep.

The smell of strong coffee wakes me in the morning, and I open my eyes to the dusky first light. The sun has not risen, but I jump up, excited to continue our journey. If all goes well, I will be home in five or six days. A cup of hot coffee takes away the chill from the night, and after everything is packed up and the horses are hitched, we are off again.

This time, when I cross the Tombigbee, I'm not afraid I'll drown, and I laugh at the childish thoughts I had when I first crossed the river. The horses splash in the chest-high water as Floyd and Luke coax them onward.

When we stop for a break in the early afternoon, I ask young Luke if I can ride up front with him so I can see the scenery. I remember how beautiful it was on my first journey. He blushes, which I find endearing, but he nods and allows me to climb up front. When I step up on the frame of the wagon, he puts out his hand and offers to help me up.

Luke doesn't make conversation, and I'm happy for the silence. The sun feels good on my face, and I remove my bonnet to let the warm, humid breeze blow through my hair. The river is as lovely as I remember it, and I take a deep breath to smell the moss and fish and water.

As the days pass, I feel more and more comfortable in the company of the men. They're showing themselves to be gentlemen, even if they seem a tiny bit put out by having a woman on their journey.

Buck shoots something for us to eat every night, and Earl has proven himself to be a wonderful cook.

We don't eat much but meat and stale bread, but it's very tasty, and I have not been hungry for a single moment of our journey.

Following supper every night, we sit around the campfire, and Luke pulls out his guitar and plays soft music. Tonight, between the guitar strumming, the logs crackling, and the warmth of the flames, I fall asleep under the stars on the ground with the men.

When I wake in the morning, I'm not only damp and cold, I'm embarrassed that I fell asleep with them, but they don't treat me any differently than any other day. We enjoy coffee and warm up last night's leftovers, then pack up our belongings and head out for another long day.

As we distance ourselves from the winding river, I remember it took two days to reach it from Mississippi, so I know we're getting closer. I ask Luke if we have crossed the Mississippi state line yet. He thinks we may have. I watch the horizon begin to disappear into the woods as the pine trees become denser, and I know I'm almost home.

We stop for the night when the sun starts to set, and Buck heads out to find us some supper. After starting a fire, Luke sits down and strums his guitar. I watch him play, thinking how grateful I am for his help. Earl stirs a kettle hanging above the fire, then sits down on a log and whittles a piece of wood. I don't see Floyd anywhere. He's probably taking care of some personal business, so I don't question it, but when he appears back at the campfire, stumbling with a whiskey jug in his hand, everyone stops and stares at him. The air becomes icy. Suddenly I realize all the men know something I don't.

Earl pipes up with the first words I have heard

from him in six days. "Floyd, what the hell are you doing?"

Floyd staggers over, kicking up dust in his drunken shuffle, and almost falls on top of Luke. He stumbles and lands on the ground near the log Luke is seated on. Floyd rolls onto his back, then wobbles back up to a sitting position. He takes a long slug from his jug and lets out an "Ahh."

He turns to Earl. "Shhut up, Earl! It'sh none of yer damn businessh," he slurs. He then leans toward Luke. "Play shomething good. I wanna hear shomething good." He throws his head back and takes another swig from the jug.

Earl rises from his place on the other side of the fire, casually walks over, and sits next to me on a log. He whispers in my ear, "Don't worry about him. Let him finish the jug and he'll pass out somewhere." His words are comforting but there's something in his tone that sounds tense and edgy.

I don't acknowledge his words, because Floyd is now staring at us and trying to get back on his feet.

"What are you whishpering ovah there? Are you trying to keep that pretty little girl all to yourshelf?" Floyd has risen to his feet, with more than a little difficulty, and is staggering toward us. He stops for a moment in the middle of the campfire clearing, and guzzles from the jug, throwing his head all the way back. I think he may fall backward, and I wonder if he will break open his skull if that happens.

Earl doesn't move from his spot next to me. He sits in a relaxed pose, leaning forward with his elbows on his knees, with a half-whittled piece of wood in one hand and a knife in the other.

"That's enough, Floyd! Go sleep it off." His

stern voice doesn't match his calm body language, but when I see his eyes squinting in Floyd's direction and his jaw throb with anger, I think Floyd should do as he is told.

"Don't tell me what to do, Earl. I wanna talk to the pretty girl, too."

I don't move. I don't even think I'm breathing. I have never seen a person in this condition before, and I'm not sure if he's dangerous or if he's going to fall down at any moment.

Earl slowly rises to his feet, moves in front of me, and lowers his voice. "You're not going to do any such thing. The lady doesn't need to speak with you when you're drunk."

Floyd wildly takes a swing at Earl and hits him right in the jaw, causing Earl to hit the ground with a thud. He is out cold. Luke throws his guitar down on the dirt, runs around the outside of the circle, and grabs for my hand, but Floyd beats him to it. Before I realize what is happening, Floyd spins me around and I find myself facing Luke, pinned in Floyd's arms.

"That'sh better, pretty lady," Floyd slobbers. The rancid odor of whiskey and rotting teeth invades my nostrils.

Luke freezes and pushes his hands toward the ground in an attempt to calm Floyd down. "Look, Floyd, you don't want to do this."

"How do you know what I wanna do?" He spits down my neck as he speaks, wobbling back and forth. The motion and the smell are making me sick to my stomach.

Luke looks past me, over my shoulder. He nods, then there is a sudden noise behind me, and Luke grabs my hand and says, "Come on!"

"Hey!" Floyd hollers at us as we pull away.

"That's enough, Floyd!" Buck yells, appearing from the woods behind us.

Floyd turns toward Buck, and moves faster than his inebriated body should be able to. As Floyd loosens his hold on me, Luke yanks me toward the wagon and shoves me in. Buck grabs Floyd by his outstretched arm, spins him around, and puts the knife up to Floyd's throat. Floyd curses, demanding Buck to let him go. I assume Buck refused, for they're soon having an all-out brawl. I hear the jug hit the ground, but I don't know if Floyd threw it or dropped it. I also hear fists making contact with flesh. I can't imagine Floyd is in any shape to fight off a man like Buck.

I jump when I hear a gunshot. Everything is abruptly silent. The bullfrogs stop croaking, and it seems as if time is standing still. I look wide-eyed at Luke, wondering if Floyd has been shot.

"It's all right," he says, shaking his head in answer to my unspoken question.

"Are you sure?" I whisper.

He nods. "Yes. I'm sorry. We were hoping Floyd would stay sober, especially with a lady around."

I hear Buck order Floyd to lie down right where he is and sleep it off, and I breathe a sigh of relief that Floyd is still alive. I don't hear another word from either man, so I assume Floyd did as he was told.

Luke leaves the back of the wagon. I don't move. After a few minutes that seem like an hour, he comes back and says, "Floyd has passed out by the fire. You're safe now."

"Thank you. I didn't know I wasn't safe before," I mumble to him.

"You should get some sleep now." He disappears.

I stare at the back of the wagon, wondering if I should go check on Buck or just do as Luke said. My heart is pounding out of my chest, and I don't think I could sleep if I tried. I sit and listen for any sound from outside.

I jump as Buck appears around the back of the wagon. I didn't hear him approach. "Are you all right?" he asks.

I nod.

"I'm very sorry, but it's over now." He sits next to me and takes my shaking hand in his.

"Thank you for protecting me."

"You're very welcome. You get some sleep and I'll see you in the morning."

"Is he going to sleep all night?" I point my thumb in Floyd's general direction.

"Yes, you'll be fine. I'll be right here outside your wagon all night." My pulse is racing, but Buck makes me feel safe.

"Goodnight, ma'am."

"Goodnight."

Buck disappears around the side of the wagon, and I hear him slide down and lean against the wagon wheel. I hate the thought of him sleeping there all night to protect me, but am grateful he's doing so. I now realize why Buck is here, and think this is an odd use of a sharpshooter. Once I relax, I have no trouble falling to sleep, knowing Buck is only a foot away.

The next morning is deadly quiet between the traveling companions. As I exit the back of the wagon, Buck hands me a cup of coffee and inquires as to how I slept. I assure him I slept well and thank him again for watching out for me. No one else says a word about last night. Floyd climbs up to the driver's seat on the front wagon like nothing happened, and we're once again on the trail. I, however, have been asked by Buck to make myself comfortable in the back of Luke's wagon, and I intend on staying there until I get home.

By late afternoon, I arrive at Lizzie's.

Sisters

When we arrive at Lizzie's house, Necie comes running out the front door toward the wagons. The last time I saw her, she was just a little girl, but now I almost don't recognize her in her dark burgundy dress, with her white apron tied over the top, and her beautiful blonde ringlets in a long braid down her back.

I jump down from Luke's wagon, run up to her, and give her the longest hug ever. We cry tears of joy, and when we finish hugging, I push her back a little so I can look at her. What a beautiful woman she has grown to be!

"I'm so glad you're home," she cries.

"Me, too!"

Buck appears behind me and hands me my bag. "Here, don't forget this," he says.

I turn to face him and wonder if I will ever see him again. He has been a godsend. He reaches out his arms to offer me a hug. I fall into them and hug him back.

"I hope we get to see each other again someday," he mutters, the lines appearing around his eyes as he smiles.

"Me, too. Thank you for everything."

"Let's go!" howls Floyd from the front wagon.

Buck tips his hat to me as he backs up to the second wagon. I watch them drive off, then Necie takes my hand and pulls me toward the house.

There is no front porch, just two stone steps leading right to the front door. The house is quite small, with just a parlor and three bedrooms. It reminds me of Aunt Mary's old store. I feel both happy to be here and sad at the memories of being here. The parlor, with front and back doors, holds a tattered sofa, a small table with four chairs, two other chairs in the corners, and a fieldstone fireplace surrounded by cookware, oil lamps, and other necessities. Necie tells me Lizzie and David share one bedroom, the three children share the second, and she and I will share the third.

"Now, tell me everything! Who were those men in the wagon?" Necie asks as she drags me to the sofa. "Oh, I'm sorry, do you want something to drink, or would you like to freshen up first? I put some water in the washbasin in our room. I can take you there right now, if you want."

"No, that's all right," I say. "I want to see you more than I want to do anything else. And those men were hired by Uncle Hays to see me home, though it took some convincing to get him to help me."

She listens intently as I tell her all about Alabama, Aunt Elizabeth, Uncle George, and Lucrecia.

"I'm so sorry about Aunt Elizabeth. I know how hard that must have been. And what was Lucrecia's problem?"

"I don't know. I guess she wanted to be the woman of the house, and with me there, she wasn't.

It was so uncomfortable watching the children get pulled into the battle between her and me, I just had to leave. But I am so excited to be home now and to see you and Lizzie. Where is Lizzie? And tell me all that I've missed here."

Necie takes a deep breath. "Lizzie went into town with David. They'll be back soon." She pauses. "I guess the most important thing around here is Frank White." She smiles like a woman in love.

I smile back. "And who, pray tell, is this Frank White?"

"He's my beau. We've just started seeing each other, but I'm sure he's the one."

"The one? As in marriage?"

She nods. "He is so handsome. I can't wait until you meet him." She's beaming now.

"I am overjoyed for you, Necie. You deserve to be happy, and I hope Mr. White takes very good care of you. Now, when will Lizzie and David return? I can't wait to see them."

"They said they will be back by supper. I have to tell you, though, you will never get to talk to Lizzie alone. Remember how inseparable they were when they were younger? It's even worse now. They're head over heels in love and never apart. They'll be so glad you're here, though."

"What else have I missed? How is Aunt Mary?"

"She's doing fine. She and Uncle William now have three children: Alice, Ludie, and John. They sold Grandpa Hays's old house about ten years ago, and now just stay out on their farm and keep to themselves. We'll take a ride out there and visit them once you've rested a bit."

"Tell me about Lizzie's children."

"Lizzie and David also have three children. James and Mary are in school all day, so we just have little John home. Lizzie spends a lot of time volunteering down at the church and usually takes John with her, so they're not here much. And David is busy with the farm, so most of the time, it's just me. I am so glad you are here!" She leans over and gives me a long hug. Tears sting my eyes, and as she releases me, I wipe them away and give her the biggest smile I can muster.

She shows me to our room so I can wash up and change my clothes. It feels good to be clean after a whole week of living on the trail with a group of men. I come out of the room and ask Necie for a piece of paper and a pen so I can write to Uncle Hays and let him know I have arrived safely. Necie says we can go into town and mail the letter tomorrow.

I think of something else. "Have you been down to the cemetery to see Momma and Daddy?"

"I've gone down there a few times, but I'm not positive where their graves are because they have no headstones. I was only four when they died, Ellen. I don't even remember them."

"I will show you exactly where they are if you want to go down there." I pause. "You know, you look just like Momma," I tell her wistfully.

"That's what everyone says, but the only mother I remember is Aunt Mary. I don't remember our real momma at all."

"She loved you more than anything. She kept your hair in pigtails and never, ever put you down. I'm surprised you even learned how to walk." I smile at her, feeling an overwhelming sense of nostalgia.

"Do you want to go to the cemetery now? I can

hook up the horse, and Lizzie and David won't be home for a while yet."

"Yes, I would like that."

As we ride down the familiar roads, I note how some things have not changed at all, and some things look like they're from a different place. I see a few houses that were not here before, but mostly, there are empty fields where houses, barns, and farms once stood and family and friends once lived. How can everything have changed so much? I'm surprised that most of it looks even worse now than when I left.

I vividly remember the bumpy dirt road leading to the cemetery as we turn onto it, and I know we are close. I ask Necie about the general store Aunt Mary used to own.

"It's not there anymore. I think someone burned it down or something. We'll ask Aunt Mary about it when we see her."

"What about our old house?"

"It's not there anymore, either. It just rotted away after being abandoned for so long. There are still bits of wood and sections of the barn walls lying on the ground, but the house is gone."

I feel like crying; I loved our house. Daddy built it with his bare hands, and I can't believe it's gone. So many memories, so much laughter, erased from the earth.

We pass the church on the right and within a few yards, we stop in front of the cemetery gate. In the sunlight on this beautiful balmy day, it doesn't look as awful as I remember. We slowly zigzag through the headstones and head for the southeast corner of the cemetery where Momma and Daddy are buried. I remember exactly where we laid them to rest, but I look around, confused, as we approach.

"It looks like there's nothing here," I say.

"We never did put up any headstones. I guess we just never had the time or money to do it, so there's nothing but grass."

There are no crosses, no stones, no flowers. I expected mounds of dirt, and am dumbfounded that the ground is just as flat over their graves as it is everywhere else. There is absolutely nothing to tell anyone that two amazing and special people are buried here. Now I understand why Necie can't find their graves.

"Maybe we can ask Aunt Mary or Uncle Hays for help purchasing grave markers or something," I say.

"If you want to, I guess we can. I don't think anyone really cares anymore. It's been such a long time. From what I understand, a lot of people died at that time, between sickness and the war, and there are many people buried around here without headstones."

Necie and I sit on the grass for a while and reminisce about our lives with Momma and Daddy. I'm surprised by how much she doesn't remember. I feel sorry for her that she doesn't know how wonderful our parents were. Her childhood memories are so different than mine, but thankfully she doesn't carry the pain that accompanies mine. I stroll around the cemetery, wondering if it's better to have the memories and the pain, or to have never known my parents' love at all.

When the sun begins to set, Necie suggests we head back to the house. "Lizzie is probably back by now and wondering where we are."

I nod, we brush the dirt off our skirts, and head

back to the wagon. As we ride back to the house, I feel melancholy and a little nostalgic for the life we once had. It hurts so much that no one cares to remember Momma and Daddy. Maybe there just isn't much to remember. They were good people, raised their children, attended church, and worked on their land. They were not important or special...to anyone but me.

When we arrive at the house, Lizzie runs out to greet us. She hugs me and gives me a kiss on the cheek, and I'm surprised that she looks so much older than I remember. I guess we all have aged, but she has streaks of gray in her hair and her eyes look drawn and tired. Her cheekbones protrude, and I think she looks awfully thin. She's wearing a dark brown bag of a dress, and I wonder what happened to my vibrant sister who used to chase butterflies in the field.

"My goodness, you are not my little sister anymore. Look at you!" she exclaims.

"It's so good to see you, Lizzie!" I'm not able to say anything about her looks.

We spend the remainder of the evening poring over details of her children and my time in Alabama. The three of us plant ourselves in the parlor, all talking at the same time, like we haven't missed a single day of being together.

In the middle of our conversation, David enters the back door from working in the field. He stomps his boots on the rug and hangs his jacket on the hook. He warmly greets me, and I'm pleased to see the man the gawky teenager has become.

Lizzie rises, he takes her in his arms, and kisses her on the forehead. He looks down into her eyes with such love, my breath is taken away. *That* is what I want! That look of love. I got it from my mother and my aunt. I want it again, and I want it from a man.

Aunt Mary

Aunt Mary stands on her porch and waves to me as I pull up in the wagon. I journeyed to the farm by myself, because Lizzie was busy at the church, and Necie was out for the afternoon with Frank White.

Aunt Mary has aged a lot in the last thirteen years, but is as beautiful and warm as I remember. She's wearing a modest, dark blue dress with an apron on top, and her dark hair is tied neatly in a bun under her floppy-brimmed bonnet.

As I jump down from the wagon, she hurries over and then wraps her arms around me.

"Oh, my Ellen, look at you! You're all grown up. I feel like one of my long-lost children has returned," she exclaims.

"Hardly a child anymore. I'm twenty-six now, Aunt Mary." I smile at her, looking deeply into her warm eyes. I'm surprised she looks so much like Aunt Elizabeth, and even more surprised that I never noticed the resemblance before.

"Are you home for good or just for a visit?"

I shrug. "I don't really know."

"Well, come on in and I'll make us some coffee, and you can tell me all about your adventures in Alabama."

We sit down at the table with our coffee, and I tell her the whole story, beginning with the trip there and ending with Lucrecia.

"Then it sounds like you're home for good," she concludes.

"I don't know, Aunt Mary. Lizzie is a busy bee, and Necie is with Frank White all the time, so I don't really feel like there's room for me there. I don't know how to create a life that fits in with their lives."

"Well, honey, there ain't much around here anymore. After the war, the railroads opened back up, but businesses didn't come back. So many young men didn't come home from the war, and losing all the slaves made it worse. Most of the farmers just up and moved away."

"Yes, I noticed how many farms are now deserted as I rode out to the cemetery. It's like a ghost town around here."

"I don't think it will ever be the shining community it once was." She sips her coffee and shakes her head.

"How are Uncle William and the children?" I ask.

"Oh, your uncle William is getting a little slow in his old age. He doesn't complain at all, but I think his knees bother him a bit. His old legs don't move as fast as they once did. But I love him just the same." Her eyes twinkle as she speaks. "And the children are all healthy and doing well in school. I couldn't be more pleased with them." She smiles. "What about you? No boyfriend? At twenty-six, you should be thinking about children, too, no?"

"I don't know about that, Aunt Mary. Maybe it's just not in the cards for me. I think I may be a little gun-shy after what happened with Milton. I don't want to go through that again."

"Well, child, I don't think there are any eligible men around here for you. Maybe you should head out to Texas and have your brothers introduce you to one of them cowboys." She laughs, but I have a suspicion she is not kidding.

"But Necie has a boyfriend, so there has to be some men around here."

"Look at Necie. She's beautiful and twenty-one. She could have the men lining up from here to Biloxi. The rest of us aren't so lucky."

I know in my heart Aunt Mary didn't mean anything negative by her comment, but I again feel like the ugly duckling of the family. Not pretty enough to attract the attention of a man, not young enough to make a good wife. I had almost forgotten my insecurities, but they all come rushing back with Aunt Mary's words.

After my visit, I head back to Lizzie's. I pass abandoned farms, dilapidated barns, and empty fields, and I give a great deal of thought to the idea of going to Texas. I'm not done visiting my sisters yet, but it's obvious this is not the childhood home I remember, and not the beautiful life I wish for. Someday soon, I'll write Willie and Allen John and ask them about Texas.

Babies and Puppies

As I sit on the step of Lizzie's house, daydreaming about Texas and riding a fancy train across the countryside, I hear a scream from inside the house. I run in and find Lizzie in the middle of the parlor with her hands over her mouth.

"What is it?" I run toward her and look where she's looking.

"It's the new puppy David gave me. He's not breathing." She starts to cry.

I hurry to the mat by the back door and find the dog cold and dead. He wasn't sick. He wasn't an unhealthy pup. How did this happen? By his temperature, I can tell he has been dead for a few hours.

David, who also heard Lizzie's scream, runs in the back door. "What's wrong?" He looks panicked.

"David, look!" Lizzie points to the dog.

"What happened?" He kneels down and touches the pup.

"I just found him like that." Her forehead wrinkles and tears fill her eyes.

David stands and wraps his arms around her.

"Why would he just die like this for no reason?" she cries.

His face turns red. "I have no idea. I'm going to go talk to the man I got him from. Can you both take him out behind the barn? I'll bury him when I get back."

We both nod, and David stomps out of the house, slamming the front door.

I don't understand why he seems so angry. I help Lizzie lift the dead dog onto his mat and carry him out the back door. We place the mat on the ground behind the barn, and Lizzie sits next to it and examines the dog.

"Oh, no, here it is."

I bend over to see what she has found.

"A rattlesnake bite, right on the tip of his nose." She sobs.

"Oh, he was just a pup, Lizzie. He didn't know not to play with rattlesnakes. I'm so sorry."

She pets the dog for a few minutes, then rises to go in the house.

"What in the world is going on with David?" I ask as I follow her.

"Oh, he'll be all right. He's upset because he got me the dog as a present for something, and now he's worried." She's trying to not shed any tears, but I can see the frustration and hurt on her face.

"A present for what?"

"It's all right, Ellen. He'll get a new dog." She walks faster toward the house, obviously wanting to end the conversation.

I refuse to let it go. "A present for what, Lizzie?"

She stops and turns to look at me. "Because I'm pregnant." She turns again and heads toward the house.

"Lizzie? Why didn't you tell me? Does Necie

know?" I run up to her and grab her elbow.

She stops again. "I haven't told anyone but David, and I even tried to hide it from him as long as I could. Every time I tell him I'm pregnant, I end up losing the baby, so I hate to say anything until I'm far enough along to know for sure I'm not going to lose it. But he guessed, and he gave me the silly dog as a present."

"Well, that was nice of him, wasn't it?" I feel a sharp pain in my head right between my eyes.

"I know him. He thinks the dog dying is a bad omen."

"Lizzie, that doesn't make any sense. The dog got bit by a rattlesnake. That has nothing to do with you."

"Ellen, David is very protective, and it frustrates him when he can't keep bad things from happening." She pulls away and walks into the house.

I stand frozen in the yard and rub my temples with my thumb and third finger, trying to ease the throbbing headache that has come on quick as lightning. I didn't know my sister had trouble carrying children. I feel bad for her and David, and I wonder if the dead dog is indeed a bad omen.

Fortunately, after Lizzie delivers a healthy boy in October, David brings home a new puppy, so the boy and the dog can grow up together. We have a wonderful time nurturing the new little ones, and the boy becomes the glue that binds us sisters together— just like the family we used to be.

Necie's Wedding Day

"She looks like a princess," I whisper to Aunt Mary.

"She's been waiting for this day for a long time," she whispers back.

We stand in the pews, facing the back of the church, watching Necie walk down the aisle. She's dressed in a beautiful ivory wool gown and carries white roses. The sunlight streaming through the church windows shines on her blonde hair, making her look like an angel. I am so proud of the beautiful woman she has become. Her groom looks pretty handsome himself, smiling ear to ear, and the church is filled to capacity with his large family.

Following the ceremony, we have a celebration at Aunt Mary's house. It reminds me of days long ago when she and Uncle William threw parties for their children's weddings. I have mixed feelings about those gatherings. Some warm memories linger, but most of the time, I didn't fit in at those functions. I always felt isolated.

Today at my beautiful baby sister's wedding, I feel exactly the same way.

Aunt Mary comes up and sits down by me. "This is quite a party, isn't it?"

"Yes, it's lovely."

"Do you remember most of these people?"

"No, not really. The last time we had a big celebration, I think I was eleven or something. It's all different now."

"How so?"

"Everyone has grown up. All of my siblings are married and moving on with their lives. And I still don't know what to do with myself or my future. I mean, look at how happy Necie is. Do you think I'll ever be that happy?"

We watch Necie and her new husband spin around on the dance floor. They have the biggest smiles on their faces as they look into each other's eyes.

"Happiness is inside, Ellen. If you're looking on the outside, you'll never find it. You know, my momma once told me at the worst moment of my life that everything is in God's hands. I didn't understand that at the time, but she was right. Everything will work out for the best. You'll see."

She leans over and pats my leg. I smile at her, but have no idea what she's talking about. I have been searching for a place that feels like home. I've been searching for love. I want someone who will look at me the way Frank looks at Necie, the way David looks at Lizzie, the way Aunt Elizabeth and Momma used to look at me. I'm afraid I'll never find it. It's not inside of me; it's out there somewhere. All I want is a nice man, a happy home, and beautiful children, not this ghost town of painful memories.

March 1884

We move Necie's things out of Lizzie's house, and help her set up her new home as Mrs. Frank White. My little sister is now a married woman with her own home, and I am so happy for her.

I'll miss her and Lizzie, but I have discreetly written to Willie and Allen John and asked about the opportunities for me out West. As I await a return letter, I daydream about meeting a cowboy and making a new life in Texas. It sure couldn't be any worse than Alabama, and probably not any worse than here.

The day after we move Necie out, I hear back from one of my brothers.

Dear Ellen,

We would be so pleased if you would come visit us. My wife, Mollie, says she would love to have a sister to share supper with. Allen lives a few hours from us, so we don't see each other very often, but we keep in touch through letters. He bought a lot of property and keeps himself busy with that.

If you decide to come, please let me know how I can help. I looked into the train routes for you, and know that you can get to Runnels County from New Orleans on the Houston and

Texas Central Railways. I will be happy to pick you up from the Runnels County station. I also think there is a train from Mobile to New Orleans, but you'll have to check on that. Ask Uncle William. I'm sure he'll be able to get you down to Mobile.

I hope to see you soon. The invitation remains open always. Mollie sends her regards. Please give our love to Lizzie, David, and Necie.

Love,
Your brother,
W. H. Rodgers

I fold the letter, hold it to my chest, and feel an eagerness I haven't felt for a long time. I know in my heart Alabama and Mississippi are not where I'm supposed to be. Maybe Texas is my key to happiness. Maybe it's where I belong. I ask Uncle William for help planning the trip. He says it will take him a few days, but he'll arrange the whole thing and let me know the moment the travel plans are confirmed.

I tell Lizzie as soon as Uncle William has finished booking my trip, and she's very sad that I'll be leaving. She hugs me and wishes me the best.

"You've always been quite a gypsy," she teases.

"I think I'm just looking for something."

"For what?"

"I don't know. I'll let you know when I find it."

The next morning, Lizzie and David take me to Aunt Mary's house to begin my journey. Uncle William has arranged my trip and paid for everything. I would object, but I don't have any money to pay for it myself, so I'm grateful for his generosity. He's still the warm, kind man I remember from my childhood, and I love him dearly. This is certainly not the experience I had trying to get home from Alabama, and I hope the travel to Texas will be just as different. I really don't want to face any drunken wagon drivers on this trip.

I write to Willie, telling him I'll arrive March 19th, and ask him to pick me up from the train station.

Uncle William and Aunt Mary take me down to the station in Meridian. When we arrive, I am awed by the enormous size of the black steam train. I count eight cars, and Uncle William tells me five are for cargo and three are for passengers. Men in the back are loading wooden crates through the doors, while at the front, people are hugging, smiling, crying, and saying their goodbyes. I could stand here and watch them all day.

Uncle William and I hug goodbye, and I thank him for planning my trip and paying for it. Aunt Mary and I hug. She hands me my itinerary and makes me promise to write the moment I get there. She then cups my chin in her hand and says, "You will be happy in Texas with your brothers. I can feel it. Great things are heading your way. And if you need anything, I am always here for you. Don't forget that."

I smile and hug her again, long and hard this time. I reluctantly pull away and climb aboard the chugging, hissing train.

After I find my seat, I wave to them out the window, and I see my aunt wipe away a tear. I wonder if she cried all those years ago when I left for Alabama. I guess I never thought about it before. It makes me a little sad to think I didn't notice that when I left. I remember her smiling and telling me to give Aunt Elizabeth a hug for her, but that's all. I wave to her again as the train blows its loud whistle.

We slowly inch forward, the train wheezing and chugging, and my aunt and uncle begin to fade into the distance. I reminisce about seeing the pretty ladies waving from the train in York, Alabama, and realize I have become one of them. I made myself a promise back then that I would one day travel by train to a far-off land, and here I am. I smile as I look around at the interior. Yes, this is my new beginning, and I too can feel great things coming my way.

The train's furnishings aren't as beautiful as the Houston and Texas Central Railroad brochure described it, but this is only the Mobile and Ohio Railroad from Meridian to Mobile, a short ride. I pull the itinerary from my bag and read it thoroughly. It says I have a four-and-a-half-hour journey today, but there are about twelve stops, so I imagine it will be much, much longer than four and a half hours.

Tonight I'm staying at a boarding house in Mobile. Tomorrow, I'll take the Louisiana Western Railroad to New Orleans. That will be another five-hour journey, and I'll spend the night in a real hotel in New Orleans. I giggle because I feel like royalty. I'll leave New Orleans at seven thirty p.m. on the Houston and Texas Central Railroad. That's the train I have a brochure for. It says it's a luxurious train with a Pullman dining car and sleeper berths. I can't even imagine what those are, but they sound extraordinary. I'll travel all night and have a breakfast layover in Houston, go on to Waco with a supper layover, and finally arrive the following evening at six p.m. in Runnels County, where Willie will pick me up.

Thankfully, Aunt Mary wrote it all down. I don't

think I could remember all this, and if I'm not careful, I could wind up on the wrong train and end up in San Francisco. Although that would be just about as good a place as any, I suppose.

I return my itinerary to my bag, look around the car, and see there are very few people, but with every stop, it gets more and more crowded. I gently fan myself as I try to ignore the heat and oily smell. I watch the scenery pass by quickly. I don't think I've ever traveled at this speed before. I hear a small boy ask his father how fast we're going.

"Steam trains can go about thirty miles per hour," the father responds.

"Wow," says the child, which is exactly what I'm thinking.

As the sun begins to lower in the sky and the seats fill up, I start getting tired and hungry. I question if I made the right decision leaving Mississippi, but tell myself I'm just getting a little cranky. I will see my brothers soon and begin a new life in Texas. I can't allow myself to start feeling sad or confused now. I rest my head on the hard wooden back of the seat and soon doze off.

I wake to the train whistle and hiss of the brakes. A man dressed in an official-looking vest, with a pocket watch and a funny hat, is walking through the aisles, saying, "Mobile, next stop, Mobile. Everyone must exit the train when we stop." He repeats it over and over, and there is a flurry of activity as passengers begin chatting and gathering up their belongings.

I reach down between my feet and pull my heavy bag up onto my lap. I packed as much as I could into the bag. I know it's barely enough to visit with, much less to move with, but fortunately Uncle William gave me some money and told me to buy whatever I need when I get to Texas. When we come to a stop, I patiently wait as other passengers exit.

When I emerge onto the platform, it's already dark. I ask an official-looking white-haired gentleman how to get to the boarding house written on my itinerary. He points and says it's about a half mile down the road. I struggle with my heavy bag as I head in the direction he pointed.

I'm amazed how a town such a short distance away can look so different than my town. Many of the buildings have lights on inside, and I realize they're electric lights. Meridian has a few buildings with electric lights, but I have never been in any of them at night. Many people are walking between the center of town and the train station. It's strange to see people milling about the street like it's the middle of the day.

When I reach the boarding house, I'm surprised it looks just like a regular house. I don't know what I expected, but this is quite lovely. It's painted white and has two stories, with a long front porch and a large red sign on the door with gold letters that say, "Welcome! Please Come In." I step onto the porch, tap on the glass of the door, then try the handle. It's open, so I enter.

A charming white-haired woman approaches the door. "Hello. May I help you?"

"Yes, ma'am. I am Ellen Rodgers. I believe I have a room reserved for the night."

"Why, yes, Miss Rodgers, please come in. Your uncle informed me you would be arriving this evening."

She turns her attention to a young lad and instructs him to take my bag up to my room.

"Miss Rodgers, would you care for some tea and cookies?"

"That would be lovely, thank you."

After an enjoyable evening, a good night's sleep, and a filling breakfast, I head back to the station to board the New Orleans-bound train.

It's about the same as the last train—crowded, hot, smelly, and dirty. I wish I could get on that luxurious train I read about, but it will not be today. We chug away from the station, and I relax, knowing I have another long day ahead of me.

I pull out my itinerary to see how many stops we'll make today. It looks like only eight or so. Maybe this day won't be so bad after all. Strangely, I'm happy to be moving again, for I felt like I was moving all last night even though I was lying still in bed.

I look out the window and start getting drowsy. Suddenly my eyes pop wide open. Blue water as far as I can see!

A young man sitting in front of me turns and says, "Isn't it beautiful?"

"Yes, yes, it is! What body of water is that?" I ask, hoping I don't sound too stupid.

"That's Mobile Bay. I make this trip about once a month and I never tire of seeing it. Have you ever been on this train before?"

"No, sir. This is my first time."

"Well, you are going to love it. We're going to ride down the coastline, and every now and then, you'll get a glimpse of the Gulf of Mexico. When we get closer to New Orleans, we'll cross a long bridge over the water. It looks like you're skimming the top of the water. It's quite an experience."

"That sounds so exciting. Thank you for telling

me. I didn't know what to expect."

"Oh, you are most welcome, ma'am. If you have any questions, just let me know."

Though I get tired along the way, I refuse to close my eyes and miss any of the sights.

At our last stop before the bridge, a drunken man enters my car. He's loud and overly friendly. I really don't want to talk to him, so I'm relieved when he stops to talk to someone a few rows ahead of me. The conductor approaches him, and after a few words, the conductor grabs the man by his lapels and tosses him off the train. The man rises from the tracks and shakes his fist at the conductor, who just closes the door, straightens his vest, and apologizes to all of us. I giggle as I think of Buck and Floyd, and am relieved that this encounter ended as well as that one did…at least for us.

We arrive in New Orleans at sunset. I emerge from the train onto the platform and witness hundreds of people milling around, chatting and hugging. It's like a party right here on the tracks. I ask the young man who was sitting by me if he knows where the hotel is. He points to the train station. I look up and see a gigantic building with a dozen windows across the front, every upstairs window aglow. The sign at the top of the door reads, "Central Station and Hotel." A little embarrassed, I thank the young man and head into the building. It's a railroad station with a hotel upstairs, and it also has a restaurant downstairs. I check in at the desk, drop my bag off in my room, and head back down to get something to eat. The entire building has electric lights, fancy carpets, and the restaurant has musicians playing on a little stage in the corner. I have never seen anything like this, and it takes my breath away.

My train won't depart until seven thirty p.m. tomorrow night, so I'm excited about spending the day in New Orleans and seeing the sights. When I wake in the morning, however, gray clouds are hanging low, threatening rain. The entire day is a washout, and by suppertime, I am more than ready to climb back on the train and leave this dreary rain. I have done nothing all day except read the paper and watch the people. I sat in the train's waiting area for hours, watching the time creep by like cold molasses.

A large group of us wait in the rain for a uniformed gentleman to tell us which cars to board. It seems there are a lot of immigrants riding, and I remember seeing in the brochure that immigrants are allowed to ride for free. Maybe Uncle William should have booked my passage as an immigrant. As the uniformed man calls names, all of the women and children head to the last three cars. Men traveling alone are sent to the front two. After the scene with the drunken man in Mobile, I'm please to not have to deal with men on this train, yet I wonder how well behaved all these children will be. I hope they don't cry all night.

When the rest of the passengers are finally allowed to board, I find my car is well worth the wait. This is not like the other two trains I rode. It's comfortable and beautiful and more than lives up to its description in the brochure. The inside of the car is luxurious, with expensive cloth covering the seats, and gas lanterns hooked up high on the walls. Uncle William must have paid quite a sum for me to travel in such style.

We travel all night, and the sleeper car is just as

ritzy as the rest of the train. I sleep like a baby with the gentle rocking of the train, and wake refreshed and ready for a new day. We arrive in Houston at seven a.m., and have three hours to eat breakfast before we depart again. I have some coffee and rolls at a little café next to the station.

As we depart the Houston station at ten a.m., I think of Aunt Loucinda. She would certainly give me a lecture if she knew I was traveling on a Sunday. I snicker at the thought of her being upset and wonder how she and her family are doing. I watch the passing horizon from my comfortable seat, and think of everyone left in Alabama and Mississippi. I hope Aunt Mary is correct, that this is my new beginning.

We arrive in Waco about seven p.m. and have a layover for supper. I venture to the little restaurant next to the station, and order some food I can't pronounce on something called a tortilla. I hear people at the next table speaking in a foreign language but have no idea what it is. I suspect they are Mexicans since I know we're close to Mexico. Their beautiful children are dark-skinned, with black hair and eyes. I hope I won't have to learn a new way of speaking in my new home, though the dark-haired gentlemen surrounding me certainly are handsome.

The last leg of my journey begins with the train whistle announcing our departure from Waco. There will be many overnight stops, but tomorrow evening, I'll be in Runnels County, Texas. Willie will be there to pick me up, and we'll make the long journey to his home in Winters.

It starts raining as I walk to the train. Waco has a small station with no waiting area or refreshment area, so I stand under a dripping eave while waiting for the passenger cars to be unlocked. By the time the conductor comes around to open the doors, I am soaked to the bone and hope I don't come down with a cold.

As I'm boarding the train, I hear a man's voice behind me. "Ellen. Ellen Rodgers!"

I turn around and see a decrepit old horse, and a wagon that looks like it has seen better days. A man steps down from the wagon. He looks about fifty years old, and I almost don't recognize him, but yes, it's my thirty-year-old brother who I haven't seen since he was twelve. His hair is graying, his beard is long, his face is weathered with hard lines around his eyes. He removes his hat and smiles as he approaches me. I step down from the train, excusing myself to the people behind me waiting to board in the rain, and I run to my brother.

"Willie! What are you doing here in Waco?" I exclaim as I place my bag on the wet ground.

"I'm sorry to startle you. We had some bad business yesterday, so I was hoping to catch you here before you left." He wraps his arms around me and kisses me on the cheek.

"What happened? Is Mollie all right?" I pull back from his embrace.

"Yes, well, no, her mother died yesterday." He hangs his head, and raindrops drip from his soaked hair.

"Oh, no. What happened? That's awful."

"She's been ill for some time, and we were at her home taking care of her. She only lives a day from here. I knew you would pass through Waco tonight, so I rode like the wind to catch you and pick you up here. I traveled all last night and today. Please forgive me for not looking presentable."

I laugh and hug him again. "I'm sure I don't look so presentable myself in this soggy dress." Just as I finish my sentence and hold up my wet skirt, it stops raining. We both look up at the sky, then back at each other, and laugh. "Well, I'm glad you're here. Do you think I can change into some dry clothes before we leave?" I giggle and wipe the rain from my face.

"Of course." He smiles. "I'm so glad I got here in time to catch you." He glances at the closed station and back at me.

I can read his mind. He's wondering where I can change. "Let's go to the restaurant I had supper in. Perhaps they will let me change clothes in the back."

He picks up my bag and says, "Lead the way."

I take his arm and we walk to the restaurant, where I replace my soggy dress with a dry one. We then head back to his wagon for our journey to his house.

"Tell me all about your girls," I say as he helps me up into the wagon.

He clicks his tongue to make the horse go, and starts telling me about his farm and his wife and two daughters. He doesn't stop for the next three hours. He's much more of a talker than he was when he was a small, shy boy, and I'm tickled at his chattiness. When the full moon rises, we stop and spend a couple hours sleeping under the stars and letting the horses rest. We spend the entire next day talking about everything we have each been through for the last eighteen years, and in the evening, we finally arrive at our destination—his wife's childhood home.

Sam Meek

We stop in front of a quaint home with a white fence running all around the property. I can see by the light of the moon there are horses grazing in the pasture, and I can smell the fruit trees in bloom. The front of the house is lovely, with a long covered front porch that runs the length of the house. Willie grabs my bag from the back of the wagon and escorts me up the steps.

The front door flies opens, flooding the porch with light, and Mollie comes out to greet me, wiping her hands on a kitchen cloth. She's a beautiful woman with dark hair and green eyes. Even though she has sharp, chiseled features, she looks soft and approachable at the same time. She's wearing a dark gray dress with a faded yellow apron, and her hair is pulled neatly into a braid. Though Willie told me Mollie is twenty-five years old, she looks quite a bit older. I imagine since her mother became ill, she has not slept well.

"Ellen! Welcome! We're so happy you're here." She smiles and gives me a hug.

"Mollie, it's so nice to meet you, and I'm terribly sorry about your mother."

She thanks me, then takes my arm and escorts

me into the house.

The inside is as charming as the outside. A blazing fire warms the room, and the air smells of freshly made coffee. Mollie introduces me to their daughters: Minnie, who is five, and Willie Jo, who is two. What cute little girls! Judging by their nightdresses, they were about to go to bed. They both run up and wrap their arms around my neck as I bend down to say hello.

"Aunt Ellen, how long did it take you to get here?" Minnie asks.

"A couple of days. I traveled on three different trains."

"Did you bring us any presents?" Willie Jo asks.

I laugh. I didn't even consider doing so, but I pull two pieces of candy from my bag and they're happy with that.

I'm so wrapped up in the little girls, I don't even notice him sitting quietly at the table.

"Ellen, I'd like to introduce you to my brother. This is Sam Meek."

The man rises from the table to greet me, and I'm immediately taken aback by his rugged good looks and warm smile. Our eyes meet and lock. Suddenly I feel as if I'm drowning in a pool of green—the richest green of a mountainside, the darkest green of the deepest water. Everyone and everything else disappears.

He offers me his hand as I rise from the floor. "It's very nice to meet you."

"And you, sir." I take his hand and feel electricity flow through every vein in my body. I pull my hand away, and just as quickly regret the action. I wish to feel that sensation again, but there is no way to touch him again now. I glance down and admire his tan forearm, half covered by his rolled-up sleeve. "I am very sorry about the loss of your mother," I offer as I try to compose myself.

He doesn't respond for a moment, and stares deeply into my eyes. "Thank you. It's very sad for all of us." He doesn't pull his eyes away.

Mollie brings some coffee to the table, breaking the spell Sam Meek has created, and she motions for us to have a seat.

"Would you like something to eat?" she asks.

"No, thank you." I shake my head, finding it hard to look away from the exquisite creature in front of me.

"Sam?"

"No, I'm fine, but thank you," he says, not breaking our gaze. "I'll have to get to sleep in a little bit. I'm exhausted."

I sink into the chair but have no idea if I'm actually sitting. The thought of him leaving the room is disheartening, and I'm surprised a man I just met is having this kind of effect on me.

"So, how was your trip?" He turns toward his coffee cup as Mollie fills it.

"It was amazing. When I was younger, I traveled through a small town in Alabama that had a train station. I was so enchanted by the women in their fancy hats coming and going, I vowed to myself I would someday travel on a train to a distant place." I smile. "And here I am."

"Sounds nice." He takes a sip of his coffee, watching me over the brim of his steaming cup. His voice sounds like silk.

I watch the way he sips. I watch his strong,

callused hands place the cup back down on the table. I watch his tongue lick a stray drop from his lips. I watch his tanned throat as he swallows.

"Did you sleep on the train or did you stop somewhere?"

"I spent the night in Mobile and New Orleans, but the rest of the trip was on a sleeper train that had bunks. The rocking motion of the train was actually very soothing." I sip the strong, bitter coffee, then glance at him as I place the cup back on the table.

"Well, I'm glad you had a good journey." He stands. "I'm sorry to interrupt our coffee and conversation, but I really need to get some sleep. I can hardly keep my eyes open. It's going to be a long day tomorrow with the funeral and all." He grabs his hat from the side table. "Relatives have been coming into town all day." He nods to me. "It was a pleasure to meet you, ma'am. I'd love to speak with you more about your journey, and I'll see you again tomorrow."

"Nice to meet you, too, Mr. Meek." His movements are like a stallion running through a field, like an eagle catching its prey, like a…

"Please, call me Sam." He grins, showing the slightest dimple under his dark stubble. His eyes sparkle in the firelight.

I nod and smile. I can't stop staring at him.

He bids a good evening to Mollie and Willie, and just as instantly as he appeared, he is gone.

My heart is pounding in my ears. My palms are sweating. I can't seem to catch my breath. I wish I could follow him. I look down at my coffee cup and shake my head. When I look up, Mollie and Willie are both staring at me, and I blush.

"Well," says Mollie, "you two seemed to have hit

it off rather nicely. I'm glad you are here, Ellen." She smiles. "Sam was Momma's caretaker. Our father died four years ago, and Sam was the only one of us siblings who stayed here to look after her. He used to have quite a busy social life, but he put everything on hold for the last four years to take care of Momma. I'm sure he could use a friend. He's thirty, and he needs to get on with his life now." Mollie refills my coffee cup. "Are you sure you don't want something to eat?"

I shake my head and glance at the closed door, wishing Sam would come back into the room with the excuse that he forgot something.

As the first rays of sun filter into the room, I hear the girls playing in the parlor and feel butterflies in my stomach at the thought of seeing Sam again. I stretch in my bed and smile as I remember my dreams of being surrounded by a warm, green light. Why am I so obsessed with this man? He's burying his mother day, for goodness's sake. I should be more concerned with offering my help to Mollie and Willie, not ogling the stallion named Sam.

I'm disappointed to find Sam has already left the house and gone to the church, but I'm grateful I have time to fix myself up before seeing him. I dress in my darkest, most modest dress, and take extra time fixing my hair.

After breakfast, Willie pulls up the wagon and we head to the church. It reminds me of the one we attended when I was little—small and old-fashioned, with a warm, loving feel to it.

When we enter, people come up to me and introduce themselves. I feel like a celebrity. I guess strangers are not something this town experiences very often. I try to be gracious to everyone, but if you ask me after all the introductions, I wouldn't be able to tell you who is who. I know a few of them are Sam and Mollie's siblings, and there's the reverend and his wife, Laura, but I don't remember anyone else.

I'm feeling a little lightheaded from all the attention, when I feel a warm hand on my shoulder. My heart jumps as I hope it's Sam. I'm surprised he would feel familiar enough with me to touch me so publicly, but when I turn around, I'm even more surprised. It's not Sam, but my brother Allen John.

He's taller than I, but not by much. His face is covered by a dark beard, and his eyes twinkle like those of a child about to cause mischief. He's wearing a worn dark brown suit, complete with vest and tie. He looks so much older than I remember, but he still shows boyish charm in his dimples. I wrap my arms around his neck and give him a long hug.

"You are all grown up," he says. "And so beautiful." He kisses me on the cheek.

With all of the travel and Willie and Mollie and meeting Sam, it totally slipped my mind that Allen John lives only a short distance away. Of course he would come here today to pay his respects to Willie's mother-in-law.

"Ellen, this is my wife, Margaret." He turns toward a beautiful and well-groomed woman in a long navy dress and matching hat.

I reach out my hand to her. "Margaret, it's so nice to finally meet you."

"Likewise, my dear. I hope we'll get to spend

some time with you. Promise me you will come out to the house and stay for a few days."

"I would love that. Thank you for the invitation."

We hear the reverend at the pulpit clear his throat, so we nod at each other and sit in the pews.

The service is very pleasant. A few people take turns honoring Mollie and Sam's mother. Apparently, she was deeply loved, and I'm sad I didn't get the chance to meet her. Toward the end of the service, Sam rises and walks to the podium to deliver the eulogy. He walks with a grace that can only be carried out by a creature of solid muscle. I shake my head to bring my thoughts back to the funeral service and away from Sam Meek's muscular legs.

His words are kind and thoughtful, and it's obvious he loved his mother very much. His eyes turn dark as the sky before a tornado as he struggles to keep his tears in check toward the end of his tribute, and I feel an overwhelming desire to wrap my arms around him and take away his pain.

Why am I feeling this way? I've never been so shamefully attracted to anyone like this.

Through the entire church service and the one at the cemetery, I can't take my eyes off him. He is even more handsome in his black suit and white crisp shirt than he was yesterday sporting his rugged wool shirt. I'm a bit ashamed of how I'm staring, especially at the man's mother's funeral, but I just can't help myself. I stand on the grass and watch him across the grave, and I don't care if the whole world sees me.

Following the funeral, I'm giddy as a schoolgirl when Sam approaches me. "I'm sorry I didn't get to see you this morning."

I look into his eyes and again feel the electricity

between us. "I know you had important things to do today. Please don't apologize."

"May I make it up to you?"

"Well, I…" His mere presence renders me speechless.

He smiles. "Please join me for coffee. We can go to the restaurant in town. Plenty of people will be there, so it'll be completely proper."

I wonder if it's proper for him to be out socializing following his mother's funeral, but I guess he's old enough to make that decision for himself.

"Well?" he asks.

"Yes, I would love that."

Sam promises Willie he'll see me home safely and offers me his arm. He escorts me to his wagon and gently helps me up into the seat. We drive quietly for a while, with me watching his able hands leading the horse.

Finally I break the silence. "Sam, I'm sad I did not get to meet your mother. From the people speaking so kindly of her at the funeral, it's obvious she was very loved and admired."

"Yes, she was special. She would have liked you."

What? Do I get her stamp of approval from the grave? I can't breathe.

He doesn't say another word for the rest of the trip. When we arrive at the restaurant, the waiter greets Sam with a friendly smile and says, "I have your table ready, Mr. Meek." He shows the way and Sam nods for me to follow. A table is ready? How long has he been planning this date? That's what it is, right?

After we take our seats and order coffee, I gaze at him, wondering if I should speak or wait for him to initiate the conversation.

I break the ice. "Can I ask you a question?"

He nods as our coffee arrives.

"Did Mollie say your father has passed also?" I ask.

"He died four years ago."

"So, you're an orphan like me."

He looks at me. "Yes, I guess I am. I hadn't thought about it."

"I've been an orphan a long time." I sip my coffee and look toward the window at the people walking along the road. I can feel him staring at me.

"I guess I knew that. Willie never mentions your parents. How long have they been gone?"

I look back at him and again notice how handsome he is. I quickly look down at the table, trying to remember what he just asked me. "They died of typhoid fever when I was nine. Willie was about seven at the time."

"I didn't know it was that long ago. So you and Willie are close in age?"

"Yes, I'm two years older than him."

"I had an older sister also. Arminta was two years older than me, but she died when I was six."

"Oh, how horrible!" I wipe the corners of my mouth with the napkin.

He nods. "So, who raised you after your parents died?"

"We all stayed with our aunt for about four years. Then Willie and Allen John moved here to Texas."

"Did you stay on with your aunt?"

"No, I moved to Alabama."

He looks surprised. "Alabama? How did you end up there?"

"That's a long story, but the short version is, I went to live with another aunt. After a while, I found Mississippi just too depressing. After my aunt in Alabama died, I moved back to Mississippi. I was only there for a few years. Things just didn't feel right there, like it wasn't home anymore." My mind wanders for a minute, wondering how much I can really explain, because I don't understand much of it myself.

"I've never been anywhere but here. I've spent my whole life in this town, in that house. You've led a very exciting life so far, Miss Rodgers." He narrows his eyes at me and purses his lips in the most inviting way.

"Please, call me Ellen."

"If you insist. So, what made you come to Texas, Ellen?"

The sound of my name on his lips is distracting. "I just came for a visit." I sip my coffee.

"How long do you plan on staying?" he asks.

I pause. "I don't know. I don't really have any plans." Though my statement is true, I suddenly realize I'm desperately hoping he'll give me a reason to stay. I wait for him to respond. But I just met this man yesterday, and he buried his mother today. Am I expecting him to proclaim his undying love for me right here at this table? I look back toward the window.

"Ellen?" He draws my attention to him. "I hope you stay for a while. I would like to get to know you better."

I smile and look into his eyes for what seems like forever. Finally I look down and take another sip of coffee, feeling him watching my every move. I find his attention exhilarating.

"Well, we'd better get back," he says. "I've been so busy for the last few days with the funeral, I've neglected the farm and have a demanding schedule ahead of me tomorrow. If you're finished with your coffee, I'll be happy to see you home now." He rises.

I nod. "Yes, I'm finished." I start to push my chair away from the small table, but he's behind me in an instant, offering his assistance.

The ride back to the house is very quiet. On one side of the wagon, the setting sun is turning the sky into ribbons of pink and gold. On the other side, the darkening sky is beginning to show the first stars. I'm enjoying the expansive horizon, lost in thought. I'm torn between wanting to spend the rest of my life staring into Sam's eyes, and being afraid of looking like a foolish, lovesick schoolgirl. I want to be next to him every moment, but think I should keep my distance for the rest of my visit. I wonder what he's thinking.

The wagon is so narrow and I'm sitting so very near him, I can feel the heat from his body. As we turn a corner, his thigh touches my leg and my stomach does flip-flops.

When we arrive at the house, Sam comes around to my side and helps me down. His strong arms make me feel safe and secure. When I'm on the ground, he does not release my hand, but holds it for a few moments.

"Thank you very much, Ellen, for going to coffee with me. Maybe we can do it again sometime." He is so close, I can feel the heat of his breath.

"I would like that very much." I wish he would walk me to the door. I wish he would take me in his arms. I wish he would kiss me.

"I have to turn this horse out. Please tell Willie and my sister I returned you safely as promised."

"I certainly will."

He walks me to the steps and releases my hand.

"Good evening, ma'am."

"Goodnight, Sam."

He turns and walks back to the wagon. I don't move. God, I wish he would come back and kiss me. I wait, admiring how he hops right up onto the wagon with no effort. He touches the rim of his hat and nods. I smile and nod back. He then snaps the reins and rides away.

After he has disappeared around the corner of the house, I sigh. How can one fall in love with someone in such a short amount of time? "Yes," I whisper. "I am in love with Sam Meek." I turn and go into the house.

To Willie's

We spend the next three weeks helping Sam clean out his mother's things. Mollie and I sort through her clothes and give most to the church to distribute among the needy. Our days are busy with cleaning and cooking and taking care of the girls. Our evenings are spent playing cards, telling stories, and enjoying the spring evenings with the men on the front porch.

Sam's every move captures my soul. When he's near me, I always find him watching me. When he is not near me, I always find myself searching for him. He has totally enchanted me and I am head over heels.

I'm troubled and distressed when Willie announces it's time for us to head back to his house. I follow him outside and find him packing his and Mollie's things into the wagon.

"How far away is your house?" I ask nervously.

"It's quite a ways. About nine days."

My brain screams, "Nine days?" but my mouth won't open. I can't move nine days away from Sam. What if I'm so far away, he loses interest in me? My heart races as I try to figure out what to do to stop this.

Willie sees my reaction, stops what he's doing, and approaches me. He speaks to me in a soft tone, as if trying to calm a toddler and avoid a temper tantrum. "Ellen, I know it's a long way away, but I have to get back to my farm. We have been here for six weeks now. I can't stay any longer." He pauses. "I'm very aware you have feelings for Sam, but it's inappropriate for you to stay here unchaperoned. I'm very sorry."

I know there is nothing he can do. "When do we leave?"

"Tomorrow morning." He lumbers back into the house.

I sulk the rest of the day, and try to formulate a plan to stay. I take a walk out to the pasture to watch the horses, hoping inspiration will hit me.

"What are you doing out here?"

I turn and face Sam. "Just saying goodbye, I guess."

He places his warm hands on my shoulders. "I wish you could stay."

"I do, too, but that would be highly inappropriate, Mr. Meek."

His eyes turn dark. I've seen them do that only once before, at his mother's funeral. "Yes, I guess it would be inappropriate." He doesn't move.

One of the horses neighs and breaks the spell. I look over my shoulder at the beautiful creature. He looks like Aunt Mary's black stallion. I loved that horse. I love this one, too. I love seeing Sam ride him. "I guess you'll have to come visit me…when you have the time."

"You see how much time this farm takes. I don't know how that will be possible. I don't have anyone here to do the work while I go riding all the way across the state to court a beautiful woman." His gaze turns softer, almost playful.

"Well, Mr. Meek, we'll have to figure out something. I've gotten quite used to having coffee with you on a regular basis."

"Yes, my dear, we will figure out something. In the meantime, I have a gift for you."

"A gift?"

He reaches into his pocket and pulls out a chain, with something hanging from it. He dangles it in front of my face. A necklace with a golden heart.

"I want you to know you have my heart."

I touch the small heart as tears fill my eyes. He asks me to turn around, places the chain around my neck, and secures the clasp. I reach up to my chest and feel the heart in my hand. I turn to face him.

"It's beautiful. I will treasure it always." I throw my arms around his neck and hug him.

"My heart is now in your keeping," he whispers in my ear.

We turn and walk back toward the house, arm in arm.

While the sun rises, I help Mollie pack the rest of the girls' belongings into the wagon. When I return to the house for my bag, I stand in the middle of the parlor, looking around for the last time. This is a beautiful home, and strangely, I will miss this place more than any other I have known.

When Sam enters the back door, everything stops. I stare down at the floor and will myself not to cry. This is not my first loss. I am a big girl. I will get over it. I will get over him.

I look up and see in his face the same pain I feel in my heart. I can't bear it. I want to pull him to me and take away his sorrow, but that will only cause us both more pain, so I simply say, "Thank you for your hospitality, Mr. Meek. I hope to see you again." I nod and turn to walk out the front door. I climb up onto the wagon and tell Willie I'm ready to go. The girls start chatting excitedly, and the horses pull away.

With every mile, my resolve is crumbling into little pieces. I reach up and hold the golden heart around my neck. I have finally found the love I was looking for, and with every moment, I'm getting farther away from it. My chest is aching. I take a deep breath and vow that I will never care about anyone ever again—not that I could. When you love someone as much as I love that man, no other love can ever fill your heart.

After an hour of staring at the horizon, I swear my body is going to fall apart from the pain. I don't know how I'll get through the rest of the day, much less the rest of my life. I think I hear someone call my name, but over the horses' clomping, the wagon's creaking, and the chattering of the girls, I know I'm just hearing things.

A few moments later, however, a black stallion gallops past us and cuts off our horses. Willie yells, "Whoa!" and yanks back on the reins as we narrowly avoid a collision with the stallion and its rider.

It's Sam!

He jumps down from the steed, apologizes for stopping us, and runs around to my side of the wagon.

"Ellen! I can't let you go. Please don't leave."

I burst into tears.

Willie stands up in his driver's seat. "Sam, you know it's not acceptable for her to stay with you. She is a proper woman and you are a single man."

"Then I shall fix that." He backs up a couple steps and kneels down on one knee. He removes his hat and places it over his heart. "Ellen, will you please do me the honor of becoming my wife?"

I can't breathe. I can't see. I'm crying like a baby and can't answer him. I nod as I stand up in the wagon. He rises, grabs me by the waist, places me on the ground, and kisses me. It is a kiss like I've never known, my legs turn to jelly, my heart races. I feel his muscular chest against me. I don't want this moment to end.

The girls clap. Sam and I laugh, ending our kiss, and turn to them.

Willie steps down from the wagon, shakes hands with Sam, and pats him on the back.

"Willie, you know I'll take care of her. I would never dishonor your sister. If I may have your permission, we'll go to the justice of the peace right now."

Willie smiles and nods his head. Mollie, eyes full of tears, laughing and crying at the same time, appears beside me. "You really are my sister now...twice!" She hugs me and then hugs her brother.

Willie hugs me, too. As I kiss the girls goodbye, my brother grabs my bag from the back of the wagon and hands it to Sam. "You take care of my sister."

"I promise."

They shake hands again and hug.

Sam and I climb on the stallion, and I wrap my

arms around him as we turn back toward his home—
my home. I reach my hand up to his heart and feel the
heat from his chest.

He says we'll go straight to the justice of the
peace, but I ask him instead to go to our favorite
restaurant. He obliges and we sit down and order
coffee.

"Sam, I know it's proper to marry quickly, but I
would really like to have a church wedding. My
brother may be upset about it, but I think I'm old
enough to make my own decisions."

"Are you sure? I promised Willie we'd be married
right away."

"I would really like to get married in a church.
Please?"

He nods and smiles. "Whatever you want."

"Besides, how much damage can my virtue take
over a few short days? If anyone has anything to say
about it, let them talk."

Wedding

We can't get a date for the church for two weeks due to the pastor being out of town. But I soon realize I don't have to worry too much about my virtue, since Sam is the hardest-working man I have ever known. He works daily from sunup until sundown. He works so much, I'm surprised he's going to take time to go to the church to get married.

I don't mind so much. His farm is doing wonderfully, and when he isn't working, he gives me his undivided attention. Every day he brings me flowers and fruit from the trees. In the evenings, he plays songs for me on his guitar under the moonlight. I don't think any man could be more romantic. He plans special evenings for us and we spend many hours dining, walking, going into town, sitting on the porch. He is the most attentive man I have ever known, and he will be all mine.

On our wedding day, when I enter the back of the church, the same one we held his mother's funeral service in, I am overwhelmed by the smiles on the guests and Sam's handsome face awaiting me at the altar. I place my hand on my chest as I try to catch my breath. I feel the heart pendant under my lace neckline. It makes me smile.

I look around and think half of the county has made a showing to congratulate us. Some of the church ladies I met following Sam's mother's funeral have taken me into their fold like I am one of their own. It is so nice to see them all here today. They sit with their husbands in the pews, wearing fancy hats and smiling behind their waving fans. Of course, we chose the hottest day of the year to get married.

The ceremony is lovely, though staring into Sam's eyes throughout the sermon, I don't hear much of what the pastor says. When it's over, we exit the church to everyone's applause, and I can't wait to start my life with Sam. He is everything I ever dreamed of, and I'm the luckiest woman in the world.

We climb into the wagon and head off to our reception. Sam keeps his arm around me and leans over to kiss me every now and then.

"I'm happy you said yes, Ellen," he whispers seductively into my ear.

"Well, I have been in love with you since the moment I met you."

His eyes twinkle and I see the look of love I've been yearning for my whole life. "I love you, too, Ellen Meek. More than anything. Let's go eat!" His grin grows larger as he snaps the reins and urges the horse to move faster.

When the guests arrive at the restaurant for our reception, they all greet us with well wishes. I wish my brothers could be here, too, but getting married so quickly doesn't allow everyone enough time to make the trip.

There are so many wonderful people here, though; they almost feel like family. Laura, the pastor's wife, gives me a heartfelt hug, and the other ladies from church add their hearty congratulations. I have never felt this sense of belonging and it's overwhelming. I am now part of a community, and so excited to be a wife and, someday, a mother. For the first time in my life, I feel truly happy and blessed. Aunt Mary was right. Texas does hold my key to happiness, and his name is Sam Meek.

June 1887

"I can't believe I'm so big," I complain to Laura over our coffee. She has been my constant companion since Sam and I married. She is a blonde angel, with an infectious bubbly personality. I don't think I've ever seen her without a smile on her face, and I've never heard her utter a single complaint. She also has unlimited and boundless energy, which makes me feel like a slug in comparison, especially now, when I'm as large and uncomfortable as a pregnant woman can get.

"Do you think it will be a boy or a girl?" Laura asks.

"I hope it's a boy to help Sam on the farm, although a little girl would be nice, too." I think of Mollie's little girls and how adorable they are. I so long for a wonderful family just like hers.

"I know Sam could use some help. You can't blame him for being so work-obsessed. He provides very well for you and will do the same for your children. Men aren't supposed to be by your side all the time. That's why you have me." She grins and crinkles her nose.

"I don't know how he works so much and is here with me at the same time. He was always attentive before I got pregnant. Now, for the last few months, he won't leave me alone." I giggle and roll my eyes in pretend annoyance.

"You will never be alone. He's always going to be here for you, and so am I, and soon you will have this child by your side. You're going to be so busy with this baby."

"I'm going to be busier than you think." I smile and look down at my coffee cup. "The doctor said I'm so big because there are two."

"Two?" Her eyebrows rise.

I remain silent and watch her reaction.

"Twins?! Oh, my goodness!" With her eyes as big as saucers, she looks as shocked as I was when I left the doctor's office this morning. "Did you tell Sam?"

"No, not yet. I haven't seen him since I found out this morning."

"I wonder what he's going to say."

"He's just going to pamper me even more."

"I'm sure he will. Wow, twins! Maybe you'll get lucky and have a boy and a girl."

"Maybe. Wouldn't that be great?" I reach out and touch her hand. "You are such a good friend, Laura, and I'm so grateful to have you in my life and share this time with you."

At that moment, Sam swings open the back door, enters, and stomps his boots on the rug. I jump up from the table. I didn't hear him arrive and don't have his supper on the table. Laura quickly says her goodbyes, leaving us alone so I can tell Sam the news. As she nears the front door, she holds up her hand, fingers crossed. I smile at her as she pulls the door closed.

I clear the table of our coffee cups and put the

supper plates out for me and Sam.

During our meal, he asks how I'm feeling.

"I'm feeling fine," I say.

He shovels food into his mouth and doesn't look up at me.

"That's good," he says absently, followed by, "I'm starving."

"I can tell." I laugh at his lack of manners. After a few moments, I say, "I went to the doctor this morning." I place my fork down and wait for him to ask.

"Everything coming along?" He shovels another bite into his mouth.

"Well, the doctor said something very interesting." I wait for him to look up.

He finally notices the pause and stops eating. He looks up at me and when our eyes meet, I'm once again stunned into silence. His penetrating gaze leaves me speechless. He knows the effect he has on me, and the slightest smile touches his lips. "Well, what did he say that was so interesting?"

I blink, trying to break from my haze. "He said there are two."

"Two what?"

"Two babies."

Now he's the one who is speechless.

Finally he declares, "Well, it looks like we have our work cut out for us, then."

I nod.

"And I'd better get busy building cradles. Two. Two cradles." He attempts to process the news. "Are you feeling all right?"

"A little uncomfortable, but I'm fine."

"Good." He reaches over and takes my hand.

"Twins? You never cease to amaze me."

He pushes his chair back from the table, pulls me to my feet, and takes me in his arms. "You're going to be a great mother." He touches the golden heart on my neck, then kisses me. "I have to get to bed now, my love. Tomorrow, I have to get up early and run some sheep into town, but when I get back, I'll get busy on those cradles."

I nod. I'm used to his excessive hours, and I'm glad he's happy about the twins.

He touches the hair on my temple that has slipped from my braid, and it sends shivers down by body.

I hold him close and stare into his handsome face, admiring the lines around his eyes and the dimple on his cheek.

He kisses me again and disappears through the bedroom door. I decide to leave the dirty dishes until tomorrow, and follow him into the bedroom.

As the last two months of my pregnancy drag on, I can't believe how uncomfortable I am. My back hurts, and my feet are so swollen they won't fit into my shoes. Even though I'm nervous about delivering two babies, I am so relieved when my water breaks. Fortunately, Laura is with me. She rides down to the neighbor's house to ask them to fetch Sam from the field and the doctor from his office. They all arrive at the house within minutes.

Laura holds my hand all through the hard labor, and stays with me as the babies attempt to come into the world. It seems like I push for days, but don't feel like I'm getting anywhere.

As dusk enters the room, Laura goes out to the parlor to give Sam an update. She tells him he'll have to be patient a little while longer, but by the sound of his pacing, patience is not sitting well with him.

By nightfall, the babies are born.

They are twins. They are boys. They are stillborn.

Twins

The pastor and Laura are already at the cemetery when we arrive. She holds out her hand to help me down from the wagon, and gives me a long and tearful hug.

"This is going to be so hard," I tell her.

"I know it is. I'll help you get through it."

Sam walks around the wagon, nods at Laura, and takes my hand. His parents are buried in this same cemetery, but we haven't been out here since his mother's funeral. Over the last two days, he hasn't said anything to me about the boys or the funeral. He hasn't said a word to anyone at all. I don't know if he's sad or angry, probably a little of both.

As we walk through the headstones to the spot where our sons will be buried, I try to catch Sam's eye, but he's in his own world of pain and does not acknowledge me. He stares at the ground. I wish he would look at me.

When we get to the graves, I see Sam had a stone grave marker made that resembles an open book. One side says, "Infant born and died Sept. 13, 1887." The other side says exactly the same. We didn't discuss whether we should name the boys or not. If I had my choice, I would name them James after my father, and Joseph after Sam's father.

I stare at the marker, wishing we could have put those names on it, but it's too late now. On the bottom of the stone, the epitaph reads, "Children of S H and M E Meek. Our little boys sleep sweetly in heaven." When I read that, my knees collapse, I hit the ground, and start weeping uncontrollably. I wish the earth would open up and swallow me whole. I feel sick to my stomach at the thought of my sweet little boys under the ground. Sam kneels next to me and holds me as I bury my face in his chest.

The pastor does a short Bible reading and eulogy. How can one eulogize those who were never alive? Sam stands by my side, holding my hand. Laura stands on the other side.

All of the ladies from church brought dishes for us to take home. I'm glad I don't have to work in the garden and spend hours cooking. I only want to crawl back into bed.

Before we leave the cemetery, we place flowers on Sam's mother's grave. I don't understand how everyone can stand around talking like nothing has happened. I just want to get out of here. This place never bothered me before, but now I find it intolerable. When we finally head toward the wagon, Laura runs over to give me another hug. She offers to stop by and check on me tomorrow, but I decline her offer, telling her I wish to spend a couple quiet days with my husband.

Sam nods at her as we pull away.

"Are you all right?" Sam asks quietly.

"No. I'm tired."

"Let's get you home and in bed. I'll stay with you. The farm can wait."

When we return home, I stop cold as I enter our bedroom and see the two matching cradles standing near the foot of the bed.

Sam catches my reaction. He picks up both of the heavy cradles and carries them out of the room. I hear the back door open as it slams against the house, followed by the sound of breaking wood.

I pray this is a bad dream; I want to wake up. I wish I could take the pain away from Sam, but I'm so fatigued, I can't even breathe. I crawl into bed fully dressed, and a moment later feel Sam lie down next to me and wrap his arms around me. He holds me closely and doesn't let go. I sleep for two days and Sam never leaves my side.

Olive Lee

It has taken Sam a whole year to come around. We never speak of the boys and never go to the cemetery, but as a couple, we're healing. The intimacy we once shared has returned, and I am overjoyed to feel his love again. Therefore, I am terrified to tell him the news that I'm pregnant. I want to give him children, to fill our home with a family, but I'm frightened by the tragedy we went through last time. I pray about it day and night, and finally resign myself to allowing whatever the Lord has in store happen.

At the breakfast table, I decide it's time to face my fear and tell Sam the truth. "Sam, I need to tell you something." My whole body is trembling.

"What is it, darling? Is everything all right?"

"I…uh…" I look up at the ceiling, not able to face him. "All right, I'll just say it."

He raises his eyebrows, reaches over, and squeezes my hand.

"I'm pregnant."

He doesn't say anything. I look at him.

A sweet smile comes to his lips, and his eyes sparkle with tears. "You were nervous about telling me?"

"I just don't want to relive the last year all over

again. I can't bear the thought of losing your love."

He stands, pulls me into his arms, and runs his hand over my hair. "You will never lose my love for any reason. You have my heart, remember? Why would you even think such a thing?"

"I'm afraid you'll blame me if something goes wrong."

He places his hands on my shoulders. "Ellen, nothing will go wrong this time. What happened to the boys was not your fault, and I never blamed you or thought you guilty of anything."

"It took you such a long time to come around. I thought for a while that I lost your love."

His green eyes turn dark. "Ellen, I am so sorry. I didn't mean to distance myself from you or hurt you. The truth is, I was angry, but not at you." He pauses, looking as if he's searching for the right words, or perhaps gathering the courage. "I was angry at God. I've never wanted anything more than to spend my life with you and our children, and God took our children away, for no reason at all. After it happened, you spent more and more time at church, but with the anger I was feeling, the last place I wanted to be was at church. I didn't think you would understand it. I thought you'd be disappointed in me."

I stand stone still and listen.

He continues, "That's why I wanted a graveside service instead of a church service. At the time, I never wanted to step foot inside a church again. I'm so very sorry my anger came between us, and I promise no matter what happens, I will never allow that to happen again. I love you too much."

A single tear rolls down his face. After an entire year of fearing I was losing him, I now find out his distance and anger were not directed at me. My fear and pain evaporate as I bury my face into his chest.

After a few moments, I look up into his face and say, "I don't care who you're angry with, as long as it's not me. I can't live without your love."

"You'll never have to." He kisses me passionately.

I am so relieved when the morning sickness finally subsides, but it's replaced by fatigue, and I'm gaining weight at a record pace. I have been assured by the doctor that this pregnancy is not twins, but I sure am big as a house.

Even though I complain of being enormous, Sam tells me repeatedly he thinks I'm the most beautiful woman in the world. He dotes on me hand and foot, and brings me flowers and trinkets daily. He reassures me constantly that this child will be healthy and we'll be a happy family. I'm pleased to hear him say those things, even though I'm sure he's attempting to convince himself and alleviate his own fears, too.

If he wasn't work-obsessed before, he certainly is now. When he's not with me, he keeps himself busy with the farm and buying and selling land and sheep and cattle. I can tell he's trying to avoid worrying.

As my pregnancy progresses, the doctor restricts me from riding my horse into town to go to church, so Laura comes by regularly to check in on me. I work out in the garden a bit, but it's been so hot and dry lately, I can't stay out too long. This baby is taking every bit of energy from me, and I find myself sitting and pouting more and more.

Sam often sits with me on the sofa and touches my bottom lip with his index finger. "If you don't stop pouting, you're going to step on that lip," he teases me, trying to lighten my mood.

"I'm sorry. I'm being a baby, aren't I?"

He nods, smiling.

"I'm so nervous. I don't want to let you down again."

"We've already had this discussion," he says sternly.

"I know. I'm just afraid I'll lose this baby, too."

"Ellen, you didn't do anything to lose the boys. It wasn't your fault."

I look down at the floor.

He places his index finger under my chin and pulls my face up to meet his. "Sometimes bad things just happen. You're not to blame." His eyes touch the very depths of my soul, and I melt into them. "I love you more than life itself. My heart aches that we lost the boys, but I give thanks every single day that I didn't lose you, too. You are all that matters to me. I couldn't live without you."

He leans over and kisses me gently on the forehead. I close my eyes and then feel his warm lips on mine. I forget everything else. Every fiber in my body screams out in love for him. Everything will be fine. We will have a beautiful child. We will be happy.

On July 16, 1888, I give birth to a healthy daughter. We name her Olive Lee Meek.

March 1890

"I wish I could understand what she wants," I mumble to myself. I know not all two-year-olds are like Lee. I've raised toddlers before, yet I don't understand why I'm having such difficulties with my own child. Maybe I'm just a bad mother. I don't understand why she whines all the time. I think back to my criticism of Aunt Loucinda for not knowing why Fannie was crying, and I realize I'm getting a taste of my own medicine. Lee is such a handful. Terrible twos is a real thing.

Sam leaves before sunrise every morning. And every morning when I hear the back door close, I hope I can sleep for a few more minutes before Lee gets up. Not this morning. I hear her crying in her crib. I sleepily go to her, wrap her in her blanket, and pull her into bed with me, hoping she will snuggle up and fall back to sleep.

I wake with a start to Sam yelling in the kitchen.

"Ellen! What in the world is going on in here? Aren't you watching the baby?" I've never heard him angry before, and I don't understand why he's here or what time it is. It's barely even light outside.

"Sam?" I come running from the bedroom, tying my robe around me as I move. When I see the kitchen, I understand why he's yelling, but all I can do is laugh. He gives me a stern look, so I place my hand in front of my lips and try to stop giggling, but when I look back at Lee, I laugh even harder.

"Why are you laughing? This is not funny!" he scolds.

"I'm sorry," I mumble, dropping my head down to hide my smile. I look back at Lee, sitting in the middle of the floor, covered head to toe in flour, and I start laughing again. Flour is everywhere—the floor, cupboard, table, walls. I've only seen snow twice in my life, but it looks like it snowed in the middle of the house. I can't stop laughing.

Apparently Sam doesn't have the same sense of humor because he is furious. He stares at me like I've gone mad. The more he stares at me with that perturbed look on his face, the more I laugh. Finally, he cracks a smile.

"I guess it is pretty funny," he admits.

Lee looked like she was going to cry when she saw her daddy's stern face, but when she turns to me, I shrug and she giggles. She pats the flour on the floor, making a cloud of powder, which makes me laugh even louder. Sam shakes his head and walks out of the room.

"I'm sorry, Sam. I'll get this cleaned up," I holler after him.

"I'm sorry I yelled," he hollers back.

"I sowwy," repeats Lee.

"You should be, little girl. You have made a mess. I don't know which to clean up first, you or the house."

I start a fire to heat some water for her bath. As I place a large pot on the fire, I hear Sam come back into the house. He comes up and hugs me from behind. "You and that little girl are going to wear me out."

"We're trying to." I smile.

He kisses me on the back of the neck, sending shivers through my body. I turn and kiss him.

"I'm going into town. I'll be back soon," he says as he walks to the front door.

I watch him walk toward the door. I never tire of doing that. I allow Lee to play in the white mess while I fill the tub for her bath. This is going to take all day to clean up.

Uncle William

On March 30th, 1890, I receive a letter from Aunt Mary.

My dearest Ellen,

It is with deep sadness that I write to inform you of Uncle William's death. He died peacefully in his sleep on March 15th. Thank the good Lord he did not suffer. We have laid him to rest at Magnolia Cemetery in Meridian. The children and I are sad, but we will be okay.

Your uncle William loved you very much and always wished you the best. I hope you know that. Now in addition to your parents and your aunt Elizabeth, you have your uncle as a guardian angel as well.

Please be blessed and know that I love you. Give Lee a big kiss for me and say hello to Sam. And when you see Willie and Allen John, tell them to write to their poor ole aunt on occasion.

Love you very much,
Mary Ann Jolly

I hold the letter close to my chest, close my eyes, and picture the two of them together. They loved each other so. I know Aunt Mary is in great pain now, but I don't think she would trade their twenty-six years together to avoid the pain.

I think back to the conversation with Necie about her not remembering Momma. I wouldn't trade my nine years with Momma to avoid the pain. I will always miss her, but it hurts less as the years pass. I finally have an answer to my question from many years ago. I would rather know love and feel pain for a short amount of time than to never know love at all. Suddenly I feel more sorry for Necie than I ever did for myself.

My heart aches for Aunt Mary. "Rest in peace, dear uncle. You will be deeply missed by all who knew you."

Martha Meek

The hot, dry summer is dragging on and on, and I think I may bust with this pregnancy. Lee is such a little pistol, and I don't have the energy to run after her. She's been so much work lately, I wonder how in the world I'll raise two children at the same time. Lord knows Sam means well, but as much as he works, he isn't much help when it comes to child rearing. After the long days he puts in, I swear he is asleep every night before his head hits the pillow. I feel a little sorry for Lee that her parents are so exhausted, but I hope my energy will return after I deliver this baby. I try to do the best I can by my daughter, but right now that's not very much.

My days consist of chasing Lee around, trying to maintain some sort of clean, comfortable home, and waddling my way through this pregnancy. This wonderful life I fought so hard and long for is exhausting, and this heat isn't helping. I thought Mississippi was hot, but Texas is so scorching, you can cook an egg on a rock.

When I finally go into labor in the middle of the night on August 4th, I am deeply relieved, but I can feel something in my body is not right. It doesn't feel like the twins did, so that's a blessing, but it also doesn't feel like Lee did. I don't know what to think. Maybe every delivery is different.

When the doctor arrives early in the morning and examines me, he says the baby is not turned the right way and we need to pray it turns the way it should and quickly. He flat out tells me that a baby coming out feetfirst is very dangerous and could kill us both. After the hot and exhausting summer, his dire prediction is the last thing I need to hear.

Laura stays beside me all day and wipes sweat from my forehead. Following a one-hundred-degree day full of labor pains, I really don't care which way the baby is facing; I want this over with. Fortunately, about the time the doctor begins showing signs of his own distress, the baby flips over and begins to come out headfirst.

I push and push through the night, but we aren't getting anywhere. The doctor goes into the other room to speak with Sam. I know what their conversation is. The doctor is telling Sam that he may have to choose between the baby's life and mine.

I know Sam told the doctor to let the baby go, but when the doctor returns, I tell him if it comes down to it, save the baby. I don't think I can live through the pain of losing another child.

I wake as the sun is rising and hear a newborn's cry. Sam is by my side, holding my hand. I look into his warm eyes, and he smiles down at me and says, "It's a girl. You've had another girl. And she's healthy and fine." I'm confused as I don't remember delivering the baby, but I'm too fatigued to ask what happened. I'm just relieved it's over and we are both alive.

I whisper that I need a drink and he holds a cup

to my lips. I can barely taste the water and can't work up the energy to lift my head enough to take the drink that I know my body needs. I close my eyes and feel Sam stroking my forehead.

The next time I wake up, the setting sun is streaming through the bedroom window and he's still sitting next to me, holding my hand. His expression is sad; I don't know why. My lips feel as if they will crack if I try to say anything. I can't focus my eyes and my head is pounding. I shiver and realize I must have a fever. I doze off again.

Sam is by my side the next time I open my eyes. "Well, good morning. I hope you've had a good night's sleep. There's a little girl who wants to see her mother." He nods at someone in the doorway.

Laura appears, holding my new daughter. I wonder if Laura has been here the whole time, but I'm too exhausted to ask, and I don't know how long the "whole time" really is. I just want to go back to sleep.

Laura lays the swaddled baby in my arms, but I can't move my arms to hold her, so Laura keeps her hands on the babe. I glance down at my baby and see she looks just like Lee. I try to smile, but I'm not sure if I accomplish that.

"I think we should name her Martha," says Sam. "You never use it since you go by your middle name. Someone should use it, don't you think?"

I gaze at him and think that is a fine idea, but I'm too tired to say so. I drift off to sleep again.

The next time I wake, Laura and Sam are sitting at my bedside, talking. When they notice me awake, Laura excuses herself and leaves the room. I look at Sam and try to bring his handsome face into focus.

"How are you feeling?" he asks, trying to smile, but he looks worried, and the deep lines around his eyes tell me he's immensely tired.

I shake my head a little.

"Here." He holds a cup to my lips. "Drink some water."

I taste the water, but can't swallow. I'm freezing cold and my body starts to shiver. Sam tucks the blanket in around me, as Laura returns carrying Martha and pulling Lee by her hand.

"Don't you want to see your momma?" she asks Lee as they enter the room.

Lee reluctantly comes to the side of the bed and looks frightened. She hides behind Laura's skirt, with her fingers in her mouth. Do I look so bad that I scare my two-year-old daughter? Lee turns to her daddy, hangs on to his leg, and hides her face behind him. Well, apparently, I do.

I shiver again and fall back to sleep.

August 1890

Every time I wake, I find Sam at my bedside, sometimes holding baby Martha, sometimes with Lee on his lap, and sometimes sleeping in the chair. I feel so tired, and my stomach aches from not eating for who knows how long.

When I wake to the sun streaming through the window, Sam isn't in the chair next to the bed. He's standing in front of the window, looking out, a dark silhouette against the bright sunshine. I let out the faintest of murmurs and he immediately comes to me.

"How are you feeling today?" he asks softly.

"No," is all I manage to say.

I feel like I'm melting. I have no energy and my muscles won't cooperate. I feel a stray wisp of hair tickle my face, but I can't raise my hand to push it away.

"Why," I ask him, hoping he'll understand I want to ask, Why am I so ill?

"The doctor said it was a very bad delivery. It'll take you time to recover. You've been fighting a fever for a week."

"Sorry," I whisper.

"No, no, sweetheart, don't be sorry. You'll be fine once you break this fever. Laura has been here day and night taking care of you and the girls. You'll be fine."

I shake my head.

"Yes, you will. Don't shake your head like that." The smallest hint of a frown appears. Tears fill his green eyes as they turn dark. Seeing those eyes filled with such pain breaks my heart.

He buries his head in my chest. I try to move my hands to touch his hair, but I cannot. When he lifts his head, a tear rolls down his cheek.

"I can't do this without you, Ellen. You need to get better for Lee, for Martha...for me."

"Do the best you can," I whisper.

I feel him kiss me on the lips as I drift back to sleep.

When I wake again and glance around the room, no one is here. I look toward the window at the fading light of day, and feel the life draining from my body. I am not afraid, I am not angry. My life has been a long series of disappointments as I searched for love and a place to belong. I finally found it, and that's the only thing that matters. I found it here—in Sam's eyes. I will miss those eyes, but if the preachers are correct, I'll see them again someday, and I'll see Momma and Daddy very soon. Oh, how I've missed them.

I have never been a devoutly religious woman, but I pray now that what the preachers say is true. I trust Sam will take good care of my girls. I know they're young enough to not feel the pain of losing a parent the way I did. They'll be fine. I let it all go and place my life in God's hands.

I hear Laura have an inaudible conversation with Sam outside the bedroom door. I close my eyes. I hear Sam enter the room, close the door behind him, and sit down in the chair next to the bed. He takes my hand in his. I would like to see the love in his beautiful eyes one last time, but don't have the strength to open mine. I hope he knows I am not afraid. I hope he knows how deeply I love him.

The last thing I hear is the rooster crowing. Sam is still holding my hand, his head lying on the edge of the bed, his breathing slow and steady as he sleeps. I wish to sleep, too. I allow myself to let go, for death will be a pleasure.

Texas Christian Advocate

In Memoriam:

Died, near Nolanville, Bell Co., Texas, August 13, 1890, Mrs. Sam Houston Meek. Her maiden name was Martha Ellen Rodgers, and she was born in Lauderdale County, Miss., April 4, 1853, being at the time of her demise thirty-seven years of age.

Mrs. Meek joined the Methodist Episcopal Church, South, when quite young, being a consistent member to the time of her death. She came to Texas from Mississippi and was a resident of this state only a few years. She was joined in the holy bonds of wedlock with one of our best citizens and friends, Mr. S. H. Meek of Nolanville.

To this happy union, only a few years of matrimonial bliss were given, when grim death entered their peaceful abode and claimed the dear wife and mother as its own. It was the lot of this writer to be present at the bedside of this dying Christian lady, and witness her pure life slowly ebb away into the dark realms of the unknown future. Young, buoyant, and in the full bloom of womanhood, she was called from this earth to a higher and nobler existence in Heaven, where sorrow is unknown and death is felt no more.

As we gazed upon her placid face, perfect and resigned, we could only hope that when our time came to die, we could die as she—without a wave of trouble. She leaves behind many friends and relations who deeply mourn her loss, and her beloved husband and sweet little babies, without a mother's love to bear them on the rough and angry tide of life, for no love can equal that of a mother, which is broader and deeper than the ocean, and as faultless as the pearls that be hidden in its bed. But thanks be to God, her infant sons who passed before her are now in good hands. She will watch over them with the gentle care of a mother.

To the bereaved husband we would say, Look upward; remember the trembling faltering hand that was placed around your neck, and drawing you gently down imprinted a last farewell kiss, and among her last words, 'Do the best you can.' Never more can you enjoy sweet conversation with that loving, trusting companion, but the time will come when you too must die, and then you may meet to part no more.

> We hope to meet again,
> above in that happy home to dwell
> where all is peace, joy and love.
> We'll think of thee at morn, at night.
> When all the world is wrapped in sleep,
> when the moon sends down
> her mellow light
> and the stars their silent veils keep.

> Signed,
> a dear friend

July 15, 1986

"Good morning, Mrs. Tinkle." Betty enters the stark white room, carrying a cup of coffee. She has worked at this nursing center for a decade now, and Mrs. Tinkle is unquestionably her favorite resident.

Mrs. Tinkle lived most of her life in her own home, but her daughter found it too difficult to take care of her following a fall and a broken hip, so the daughter reluctantly placed Mrs. Tinkle in the care of these able nurses. Mrs. Tinkle and Betty have been the best of friends ever since.

Mrs. Tinkle's daughter visits every day, and apparently was here early this morning, because Mrs. Tinkle has already been helped out of bed, is dressed, and comfortably sitting in her armchair. She is staring out the window at the rain clouds that are forming on the horizon. On her lap lies a brightly colored crocheted blanket.

She turns and greets the nurse. "Good morning, Betty. How are you this morning?"

"I'm fine, Mrs. Tinkle. Here is your coffee." Betty sets the cup on the small table, within easy reach of Mrs. Tinkle. "Ma'am, there's a gentleman here to see you. He says he's a reporter from the *Abilene Reporter-News* and he wants to know if he can speak with you."

"What would a big-shot reporter from Abilene want to speak with me about?"

"He said he's doing a human-interest story on the oldest person in the area, and he wants to ask you a few questions about your life and history here in Texas. They'd like to run it in tomorrow's newspaper on your ninety-eighth birthday."

Mrs. Tinkle smirks. "Well, there's not much to tell, but I guess it will be all right." After a moment she adds, "I wonder who died and gave me the honor and privilege of being the oldest person. I wonder if I'll have to die to get them to go bother someone else." She picks up her coffee cup in both of her frail hands and carefully takes a sip.

Betty feels a bit sorry for the newspaper reporter after finding Mrs. Tinkle in such a sassy mood this morning. "He's going to have his hands full," she mumbles to herself as she leaves the room to find the reporter. She returns a moment later, followed by a young man dressed in a sky-blue, button-up shirt and khakis. He's carrying a small ringed notebook in one hand, and a Styrofoam cup of coffee in the other.

"Good morning, Mrs. Tinkle." He places his coffee down next to hers on the table and offers his hand.

She feebly shakes it and looks up at him. "Good morning, young man. What can I do for you?"

He seems momentarily stunned, but pulls his gaze from hers, slides a chair across the linoleum floor, and takes a seat. "Ma'am, I'm Bill Pickett from the *Abilene Reporter*, and I would love to ask you a few questions, if that would be all right." He digs in his shirt pocket for a pen.

"What kind of story are you writing, Mr. Pickett?"

"I'm doing a human-interest story. I heard that tomorrow is your ninety-eighth birthday, and I'd like to do a story on your life and how our town has changed in the last ninety-eight years."

"Well, I'll answer all I can, but I don't remember the first couple years." She grins at her own joke. "And I probably don't remember the last couple very well, either."

Though Bill was dreading writing this dumb human-interest story, he is so far enjoying Mrs. Tinkle's company. This might actually be fun.

"Okay, let's start with the basics. What is your full name?"

"Olive Lee Meek Tinkle, but most people call me Lee."

"And tomorrow is your birthday, correct?"

"Yes, I was born in 1888."

"Who were you married to, Mrs. Tinkle?"

"My dear husband was Fred Hanson Tinkle. He died in 1951. Let's see, that was thirty-five years ago."

"Did you remarry?"

"Oh, no, Mr. Pickett. I still love my husband to this day. No one could ever take the place of my Fred. You only have one true love in this lifetime, and no one else can fill those shoes." Mrs. Tinkle smiles wistfully.

"And who were your parents?"

"Well, my father was Sam Houston Meek. My stepmother was Nancy Smith Meek."

Bill scribbles in his notepad, then stops writing

and looks up at Mrs. Tinkle. "Did you know your birth mother?"

"Yes, of course. She died when I was two, after giving birth to my little sister. We didn't have medicines to fight off infections back then like we do now. Maybe that's one of the points you should add to your story. Women don't die in childbirth anymore, but in the old days, it happened all the time."

"What was your mother's name?"

"Martha Ellen Rodgers Meek. She was born in Mississippi and came here to visit her brothers in 1884. That's when she met my father."

"Wow, 1884 was a long time ago."

"Doesn't seem so long to me, Mr. Pickett. That's what happens when you get to be as old as I am." Mrs. Tinkle grins.

Bill keeps scribbling. "Do you have any siblings?"

"Only stepsiblings. My baby sister died two months after my mother died."

"Oh, that's very sad. I'm so sorry." He gives her a fake consoling grimace.

"Oh, don't be. I was two. I don't even remember it." Mrs. Tinkle waves her hand at him as if brushing off his comment. She then looks down at her cup of coffee. "I guess my life would have been different had my mother and sister lived, but you can't look back with regret. It'll make you crazy."

Bill stops writing and looks at Mrs. Tinkle, his eyes squinted in contemplation. "What was your life like growing up?"

Mrs. Tinkle looks out the window and watches the rain streak the glass. "My father remarried after my mother's death and they had a couple children. My stepsisters were given the best of everything, and my story, well, it's a classic Cinderella story. I was the lone stepsister who didn't get to wear the prettiest dresses or have the opportunity to meet the handsome prince." She turns back and looks Bill directly in the eye. He noticed her striking green eyes when they shook hands and is once again mesmerized by them. "I never went to the ball. Do you know what I mean?"

Bill nods, feeling he has just witnessed the secret of life, though he has no idea what she's talking about. "How would it have been different had your little sister lived?"

"Well, maybe if there were two of us, I wouldn't have been in the minority, you know? I wouldn't have been so alone."

Bill nods again, thinking maybe he's beginning to understand what she's saying. He has no idea, though, how to translate those feelings into words for his story.

Mrs. Tinkle sighs and continues, "But there is no sense in chasing fairy tales and trying to change things. No, I didn't have a perfect life, but who does? Surely not you, Mr. Pickett." She leans toward him and waits for him to speak.

"No, ma'am, I have not had a perfect life. I guess no one has." He shrugs.

"So, what are you going to do about it?" she asks. After a moment, she answers her own question. "Nothing. That's all you can do. Nothing. You have to make the most of what you've got."

The slightest grin forms on Bill's face.

Mrs. Tinkle points to his notepad. "You're not

writing any of this down."

"Oh, I'm sorry." Bill glances down at his notepad, then looks back up at her. "I'm just fascinated by your point of view. What is the greatest thing you have witnessed in your lifetime?"

After a moment, she says, "I'd have to say airplanes."

"Really?"

"Yes. Throughout my life, I've thought a lot about my mother traveling from Mississippi to Texas. In 1884, that trip must have been very difficult for her. My father told me she took three different trains and traveled for four whole days to get here. I could make that trip now in a couple of hours." Mrs. Tinkle sips her coffee. "And before her trip, following the Civil War, my uncles made that same trip by ox-pulled wagon train. It took them over three weeks. So, I'd have to say airplanes are the greatest things I've seen."

"What is your greatest regret?"

"There's no use in having regrets. Regrets won't change things, and truthfully, you wouldn't be the person you are today if you changed any of your life experiences, whether they be good or bad."

Mrs. Tinkle looks down at the blanket covering her lap and picks at a piece of fuzz. "I guess if I did have one regret…" She looks up at him and narrows her eyes. "It would be that I never knew my mother. My father seldom spoke of her so I never knew much about her. Whenever I asked him about her, he always looked so sad, so after a while I stopped asking. I have a photograph of her, but she doesn't look very happy in it, although I know people didn't smile for pictures in those days. I also have a letter she wrote to my uncle Willie in 1890. She says in it that I was two years old and a handful. Maybe she wasn't the best at parenting a two-year-old, or maybe I was a crazy child. I don't know. I'd like to ask her."

Mrs. Tinkle's face turns solemn and dark. Her eyes turn the turbulent shade of the sky right before a tornado. She looks down again at the blanket. "I guess I always felt different from everyone else. I've spent my whole life trying to feel normal, trying to belong. Everyone else had a mother, and I always felt like an outsider, like an orphan. My mother's parents died when she was a child, so maybe she felt the same way."

"When was that?"

"Her parents died in 1862, during the Civil War."

"Whoa, 1862? I can't believe you and your mother spanned the generations from the Civil War until today. That's amazing."

"I guess it is." Mrs. Tinkle gives him a soft smile and sighs. "I'm getting a little tired now, Mr. Pickett. Is there anything else you'd like to know for your story?"

"Sure, just one more question, if you don't mind. Is there anything you would like everyone to know about your life, maybe your secret for living so long?"

"I think everyone should know that you can't ever fill the holes that life burrows into your heart. You have to look for the bright things and find happiness in the little moments. Happiness is there. Love is there. Peace is there. You just need to look in the right place. I've had an amazing life. I have suffered and cried and failed and triumphed. I've embraced every moment, all the ups and downs, and in turn, it has made me the person I am. If I had grown up with my mother, I would be a different person. But, since I like the person I am, I guess everything was for the best, wasn't it?"

She turns to look out the window at the steady rain, signaling their conversation has ended. Bill rises to leave, but she says, "Mr. Pickett?"

"Yes, ma'am?"

She looks at him. "I'd like to change my answer to your question about the greatest thing I've witnessed in my lifetime."

"Yes, ma'am?"

"The greatest thing is love."

She again faces the window, watching the now-heavy rain. He turns back toward the door, and realizes he will not be writing a story about how the town has changed over the last ninety-eight years. More than likely, it'll be a story about how he has changed in the last twenty minutes.

As he reaches the door, she calls after him, "You have a blessed day, young man." She reaches up to the chain around her neck, and touches the gold heart-shaped pendant.

THE END

AUTHOR'S NOTES

This is the story of my distant cousin, Martha Ellen Rodgers Meek, as I imagine how her life was. The dates, places, and names are historically accurate, but the personalities and details of her experiences are fictitious.

An enormous thank you to family, friends, and associates who helped with research and encouragement as this book was written:

Debra Bradley Wines: fellow writer

Elyse Dinh-McCrillis: TheEditNinja.com

Jen Quist: JenQPhotography.com

Jennifer Maginn Bauer: descendant of Allen John Rodgers

Martha Wise: descendant of Martha Ellen Rodgers Meek and Olive Lee Meek Tinkle

Robert Hess: book designer

ABOUT THE AUTHOR

Lori Crane is originally from Meridian, Mississippi and is currently residing in greater Nashville, Tennessee. She is a professional musician by night - an indie author by day.

Lori is a member of the United Daughters of the Confederacy, Daughters of the American Revolution, United States Daughters of 1812, Screen Actors Guild, American Federation of Television and Radio Artists.

An Orphan's Heart was named a finalist in the 2014 Eric Hoffer Awards.

Please visit Lori's website at
www.LoriCrane.com

Bibliography

Okatibbee Creek Series

Okatibbee Creek
An Orphan's Heart
Elly Hays

Stuckey's Trilogy

The Legend of Stuckey's Bridge
Stuckey's Legacy: The Legend Continues
Stuckey's Gold: The Curse of Lake Juzan

Culpepper Saga

I, John Culpepper
John Culpepper the Merchant
John Culpepper, Esquire
Culpepper's Rebellion

Other Titles by Lori Crane

Savannah's Bluebird
Witch Dance
The Culpepper-Fairfax Scandal
On This Day: A Perpetual Calendar for Family
Genealogy

An excerpt from "Okatibbee Creek"

I can hear Charlie screaming for me as he runs up the road. He flies in the front door of the store, shouting that the Union Army is coming down the street. Oh, no, here we go. Apparently I am now in the middle of this war. Unfortunately, on this day, I have all of the children with me: my three, William's four, and James's five.

I order the boys to run to the field in back and chase the hog and the horse into the woods. I order the girls to take every jug, every crock, and every jar of food from the store and the cellar, put them in the attic, barricade the door, and stay there. Then I load my rifle. I'll be damned if I'm going to let these disgraceful, plundering Yankees ruin my life any more than they already have. And I will kill every last one of them before I let them harm the children. When the Yankees arrive, I will be more than ready for them.

I watch for them out the front window of the store. My palms are sweating. My heart is pounding out of my chest. My breathing is heavy. I can also feel my anger rising like flames from the very depths of Hell. My hands are shaking, though I don't know if it is from fear or rage. I can hear them coming before I can see them. Their horses are clomping on the dry road and there is a jingling sound from their spurs and saddles. Sure enough, they stop right in front of my store. There are three of them on horseback dressed in their blue uniforms. They are filthy and unshaven and a bit thin and weary. I slowly emerge through the doorway onto the wooden front porch with my loaded rifle in my hands.

"What do you want?" I yell to the Yankees.

"Do you have any food here?" one of them asks, though it sounds more like a demand than a question.

"No, I don't have any food," I say, surprised at the sound of the strength in my own voice even though my statement is a bold lie.

"Is your husband home?" the second one asks.

"No. You already killed him," I reply, with venom in my tone that would scare off any other man, but they don't move.

"Is there a man of the house here?" the third one asks.

"No, there are no men here, just me." I raise my gun slightly.

"You need to put that gun away, ma'am. We just want some food. We're not here to hurt anyone. You have to have some kind of food in that store," the first one says with a cocky smile on his unshaven face, as he climbs down from his horse. He removes his dusty hat and takes a couple steps toward me.

"I already told you, I don't have any food," I say slowly without raising my voice. I do, however, raise my gun to my shoulder and point it squarely at the man's face. The two Yankees still on horseback put their hands on their pistols.

The man on the ground stops moving and holds up his free hand to the other two to keep them from drawing their weapons. Again, he starts to move toward me.

I cock the hammer. Again, he stops.

We seem to be at a stale-mate. But what he doesn't know is that the rage inside me will have no trouble blowing his damn head off. We stare each other directly in the eye and neither of us moves.

www.ingramcontent.com/pod-product-compliance
Lightning Source LLC
Chambersburg PA
CBHW061146170626
46809CB00003B/996